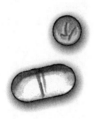

# DIAL M FOR MONSTER

a collection of cal mcdonald mystery stories

# DIAL M FOR MONSTER

a collection of cal mcdonald mystery stories

Stories by
# Steve Niles

Illustrations by
Breehn Burns
Gilbert Hernandez
Jessica Hickman
Josh Medors
Scott Morse
Richard Sala
Ben Templesmith

Cover art by
Tim Bradstreet

IDW Publishing
San Diego

idwpublishing.com

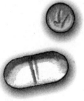

# Dial M for Monster
## A Collection of Cal McDonald Mystery Stories

Edited by Jeff Mariotte and Kris Oprisko
Book design by Robbie Robbins

ISBN: 1-932382-05-4

06 05 04 03  5 4 3 2 1

Published by
IDW Publishing
2645 Financial Court, Ste. E
San Diego, CA 92117

This one's
for my dad,
**Walter R. Niles,**
but everybody
called him Jack.
I still don't
know why.

— Steve

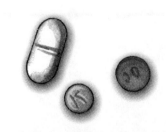

# table of contents

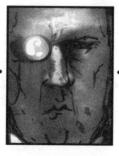

# By the time I got the call

most of the town was already infected. That's the way these things happen. If I got the calls sooner I might be able to save more lives, but I never do. The dumb fucks usually go through the usual law enforcement agencies—who of course have no clue how to handle undead outbreaks— and the problem winds up eating through and spreading.

Near as I could estimate the first zombie rose from the

dead on Tuesday, in the first week of June. By that Friday, the dead outnumbered the living, and the mayor of Mendez, California had eaten most of his staff, including his wife and twin daughters.

The place was a fucking bloodbath.

I got word of the outbreak through some ghouls, who had heard about it from a vampire fleeing the scene. Even vampires can't deal with zombies. They are without a doubt the most brainless and aggressive freaks on the scene and they'll take a bite out of anything even remotely fleshy.

The key was to move fast, before the problem spread to another town. Luckily Mendez was isolated. It was a little shit-hole west of Los Angeles. From the air (I flew over it once) it looked like a perfect circle surrounded by trees, with an outer ring of dessert wasteland. If a zombie infestation broke out, this was the place you'd want it: remote and easily contained.

I asked Mo'Lock to gather up as many of his freaky ghoul friends as he could. In the end we wound up with two busloads of dead postal workers, UPS drivers, and movie producers, packed in and ready for action. It's always easy to round up a crew of ghouls in LA. They're fucking everywhere, like rats and strip-malls.

The buses were surprisingly simple to swipe. A couple ghouls Mo'Lock knows work in a lot where they park them for repairs. They scrambled a couple of manifests and the next thing I knew I had two Greyhounds parked outside my house. Some joker had changed the destination signs above the driver's windows so they read "Straight To Hell." As soon as the sun went down I had ghouls loading in by the dozen.

For once they all listened to me and brought their own "gardening tools," as I requested. Some had axes and picks. Some brought pikes and hoes. One jackass brought a rake.

Unfortunately, no LAPD ghouls could make it.

Most of them work the night shift.


I led the convoy out of LA in my Catalina. Mo'Lock drove with me. I loaded the space between us on the front seat with some beer, had whiskey and Vicodin already in my belly and music blaring on the stereo. Mo' kept trying to talk to me as we barreled along the freeway, but I couldn't make out what he was saying over the music. The ghoul was thoroughly annoyed.

Finally I gave him a break and turned down the volume. "You say something?"

The ghoul stared at me a full thirty seconds before saying, "I asked you if you had a plan."

I lit a butt and nodded. The smoke snaked right into my eyes, causing me to temporarily lose control of the car. I swerved hard left, doing around ninety, and covered my tracks by acting like I was changing lanes. In the rearview I saw the buses keeping pace like two huge ships slicing through black concrete.

I couldn't help but imagine what would happen if they wrecked. Bodies, hundreds of them, would fly all over the highway, scattered like rice at a wedding. Only when the paramedics showed, all of them would be getting up without a scratch.

That would be fucking hilarious.

Mo'Lock repeated the question. I shrugged. Sure I had a plan. About as much of a plan as you can have when the dead are rising and devouring the living.

"I want you to get your buddies to circle the town," I said. "Form a perimeter to stop the outbreak from spreading."

"And what will you be doing?"

I glanced over at the ghoul and grinned. "I'm going in."

Mo'Lock nodded, but I could tell by the way he looked out the window he wasn't sure what I meant. Cool by me. That shut him up for the rest of the trip to Mendez.

I had the convoy stop just outside of town and gave out instructions. I wanted the ghouls to park the buses on either side of the town, and then fan out until they met up again, forming a wall of dead to contain the undead. The ghouls liked the plan. They all nodded and shook hands as they reboarded the buses with their pitchforks and axes.

As the buses drove away in opposite directions, kicking up clouds of dust, I scanned the area with a pair of night vision goggles. The good news was that I couldn't see anybody. That was also the bad news. It meant either everybody in town was dead, undead, or in hiding. I hoped for the last.

While I waited for the ghouls to set up the perimeter I went to the trunk of the Catalina and went into the "Lock and Load" routine. I took two double-barreled 12-gauge shotguns. One was sawed off, the other wasn't: for long and short range blasts. I also loaded up my .45 and a .44 magnum. I finished by weighing down with ammo attached to two ammo belts. I looked like a complete asshole.

After a bit longer than I would have liked I got calls from ghouls all around the outskirts of Mendez. The containment perimeter was in place. They were meeting resistance in the form of lumbering flesh-eaters. I told them to take them out, remove the heads if possible, and just make sure they didn't get past them.

Now it was my turn. I had to get in there and figure out how this thing had happened. There are a number of ways zombies are created, ranging from intentional creation by voodoo and all that crap, to accidental, like what went down in Pittsburgh with radiation, back in the late sixties. Once I found the reason, I could figure out the cure, if there was one. If there wasn't a cure, then we had a lot of heads to blow off.

I drove down the main road into town, passing one partially devoured body and a "Welcome to Mendez" sign. I stopped the car and got out right after the sign. If there's one place you don't want to be in a zombie outbreak, it's in a confined space. I stood a much better chance on the streets.

At first I didn't see much, just a bunch of small town, redneck bullshit like a bingo/square-dancing hall, a seed store and a diner that looked like it hadn't been painted in... well, ever.

I came across a few more bodies scattered around the streets. One looked like the local law. He wore a tan Sheriff's uniform. His head had been completely pulled off. It was lying in the street, most of the flesh ripped right off the skull. There was another corpse outside the diner, a woman and a small headless shape next to her. Her kid, I assumed.

On the streets I saw drag marks of blood, as well as drag marks made from shoes. That accounted for the lack of bodies. The zombies, wherever the fuck they were, had probably dragged the bodies off to a nice shady spot to eat.

"Hello!" I yelled. "Helloooooo!"

I listened to my voice bounce around and disappear, but nobody answered. I pressed on and looked for anything suspicious. I went inside the diner. What had looked empty outside was anything but. There were devoured bodies all over the floor, piled one on top of the other. Most of them had their heads torn off and their skin was stripped clean to the bone around the arms, legs, and some of the torso. There were a couple who still had heads. I steered clear of them, in case they came back.

Back outside the diner I sucked a lungful of fresh air and scoped the scene. It was odd. Usually these outbreaks were like zombie riots. They were everywhere. Not in Mendez, though. The place was a ghost town.

I checked the bingo hall and had a little bit of luck. There were four zombies fighting over the body of a young woman. They were tearing her to shreds, pulling and shoving and grunting. When a piece broke off, a zombie would huddle on the floor like a caveman and suck down his hunk, then get back into the fight for more.

I stood there a full minute before one of them smelled me. When it looked up and sniffed the air I stepped quickly across the floor, planted the sawed-off against the bridge of its nose, and blew his head clean off from the lower jaw up. The other three started moaning and flailing and came at me faster than I'd ever seen zombies move. I shot two with the magnum and the third with the long barreled 12-gauge.

I thought I was done in the bingo hall, but I wasn't. The girl they'd been tearing apart, despite massive tissue loss, began to move. When I glanced at her, she was gnashing her teeth in my general direction. I stared into her eyes. They were shocking: focused on me. That, and the flesh eating, eliminated any voodoo possibilities. These freaks were probably the result of someone's wrongdoing, or radiation.

I didn't want to shoot the girl, but I couldn't risk the spread so I put a .45 slug through her head. There was a bit of a spray from the exit wound, but despite the wedges of missing flesh, she looked like she just fell asleep.

I left the bingo hall knowing a little more than I did the minute before. I knew I wasn't looking for a person. What I needed to find was the location of an explosion, or some sort of radiation leak. I combed the rest of the two-block area called "downtown," then proceeded to the larger residential streets.

That's where everybody was.

The tree-lined suburban streets were littered with zombies shambling all over the place like drunks at a block party. They were eating scraps from well-picked bodies and pounding on doors of sealed up homes, so there must have been survivors. At least I hoped there were. From the looks of the sheer numbers roaming the street, I had my doubts.

I chose the most direct route and started walking right up the middle of the street. These weren't undead who were cursed or under a spell, so there was no chance of bringing them back. They had to be killed. Every single one of the infections could be passed on. This was also another reason to get the job done before the Feds or the military showed up and tried to "sample" the infection, whatever its origins, for weapons testing. What fucking idiots.

I started blasting as soon as a zombie stepped in range. The first one took the shot in the neck and kept coming. I adjusted my aim and smeared its head all over the street. As soon as I dropped number one, the whole army of dead turned and saw me.

"Come on fuckwads!" I yelled. "Time to die again!"

They came to me like ants to cookie crumbs.

Just call me king of the assholes. What a stupid move.

I took the first wave in stride blasting one, two, three and four flesh-eaters with the shotguns. I maneuvered through the shambling crowd by turning constantly as I walked, always firing. When I needed to reload, I'd kick a few out of the way and sprint to a clear area. It took the brainless dead a while to find me again, but these freaks were pretty fast. I had to keep on the move or I would easily get overwhelmed.

As I ran to a clearing near a house with a white picket fence I cursed myself for bringing the shotguns. They were effective, yes, but reloading took too long and opened me up to attack. As if to illustrate my point a quartet of dead came lumbering at me from behind the house. It was a family, the residents of the house, I presumed: father, mother, daughter and son. A family that dies together, dines together, I guess.

The boy—couldn't have been more than eleven—came at me and tried to attach himself to my thigh, but I slammed him in the face with the butt of the shotgun right as he went in for a chomp. The sister came next. The small ones moved faster. I threw her to the lawn next to her zombie brother and turned them both into ground beef with the sawed-off.

I turned my attention to mom and dad, raising a weapon toward each, but as I did I realized the crowd I'd run from had caught up to me. Suddenly, I was surrounded. Normally

I'd take a dive and bring them down at the knees, but these
were flesh-eaters. You don't want to be stuck at the bottom
of a pile with these motherfuckers. Instead I fired off some
shots and then used the shotgun like a bat and cleared a path.

But nothing I did shook them. No matter how fast
I moved, they were there, relentless and hungry. I was
probably the only fresh meat on the streets so within a few
minutes I was the pied piper of the dead, leading a parade
of slobbering zombies in a circle around the block. Every
couple of feet, when I felt like I had some distance, I'd turn
and blast the ones at the head of the procession to shorten
the line a bit.

After about an hour of running, stopping, turning and
blasting, I had made a significant dent in the ranks of the
living dead of Mendez. I reduced the small army of transformed townsfolk into a scattered mess of headless bodies.

There were still a few wandering here and there when I
spotted the thin trail of smoke rising from the trees. My best
guess was that it was the next block over. I reloaded all the
guns and then followed the trail. It wasn't much smoke,
probably a kitchen fire started when the cook got eaten or
turned, but with a pause in the living dead onslaught it was
the next best thing to a lead.

The trail led me to the next residential block. It looked
exactly like the previous—mid-range family homes, mostly
Spanish style—except this was block wasn't covered with
bodies and brains.

But it was still early.

The smoke trail seemed to be coming from the roof of
one of the few two-story homes on the street. I couldn't tell

from where I stood so I climbed on a parked car. From the roof I could see the house across the street, the smoke, and the hole in the tile it was rising from.

Bingo.

I double-checked my weapons and then called Mo'Lock to give, and get, an update. It took a couple of rings but he eventually picked up.

"Mo'," I said, "it's Cal. What's the report?

"Um... not much."

"How's the perimeter holding up?"

"Fine."

I took a deep breath. "How about some details? Have you and your buddies run into any zombies."

"No."

"Not one?" I asked.

"Not one."

I gripped the cell hard in my hand. "So, while I've been in here fighting for my goddamn life, you guys have been—"

"Securing the perimeter."

I kicked the car and put a massive dent in the door, then I threw the cell as far as I could towards the woods surrounding the town. I hoped I fucking hit one of them.

Without back-up I walked to the house with the smoke coming from the hole in the roof. The front door was wide open, and from the dirt and blood all over the front porch, it looked like there had been a lot of traffic in and out of the house during recent events.  I couldn't hear anything from inside, but a strange heat put me on edge.

I entered the house slowly, with shotgun barrels out in front. It was dark, and the blood on the porch continued inside as well. In fact, the foyer floor was so blood-covered that it would have looked like a paint job if not for the spatters on the wall and the drag marks and footprints. To my right was a staircase, not so bloody, but I went up since that's where the hole was.

The place had kind of a Victorian/*Psycho* thing going on. Lots of dark wood on the floors and walls. I plodded up the stairs to a hallway and started checking rooms. It was clear until I hit the master bedroom.

Inside, I found the hole in the ceiling.

But the hole, about the size of a large pizza, didn't stop at the ceiling. Whatever came down through the roof had kept right on falling. I walked to the edge of the hole and leaned over. From the looks of it, the hole went clear down through the ground floor and into some sort of basement or wine cellar. It was dark, and from this height I couldn't see much more than the smoke that rose towards my face, twirling and winding like a transparent snake towards my nose.

I avoided the smoke, covering my nose, and made sure I didn't inhale. Call it a hunch, but I suspected the smoke was a part of this mess. Up close it had a green tint, and it moved slower than normal smoke. Like milk diluting water. Like it had purpose.

I backtracked down the stairs to the main floor and searched quickly for a basement door. There wasn't one, so I walked to the back of the house and through the kitchen, where it looked like someone had been baking when whatever it was fell through. There were pots and pans out, measuring cups, the works.

I passed through the kitchen and went outside through a wood framed screen door. The yard was fenced in: white picket, of course. There were also clothes hanging on a line.

The scene was beginning to remind me of a Norman Rockwell painting. Well, a Rockwell painting with the living dead tearing grandpa's gut out.

To the right of the screen door was one of those *Wizard of Oz* storm doors cutting into the ground and part of the house. The door was open.

I glanced down into the cellar. It was dark, but leading in and out of the darkness, on the stairs, were bloody footprints. It looked like this cellar had been well used since the outbreak. I tore some fabric from a sheet hanging in the yard and made myself a mask to keep the smoke from getting in my nose and mouth, and then I checked my shotgun and started down the stairs.

I paused briefly about a step and a half down. There was a sound in the air, a distant flutter. It was either someone heading this way, or the wind. I didn't give a shit which.

I walked down the stairs to the cellar, pausing briefly on the last step while my eyes adjusted to the darkness. Once adjusted I could see that the basement was little more than a dug-out hole, with cement walls and floor, used to store the water heater and air conditioning unit. Over time a considerable amount of other junk had been added, including bikes, old exercise equipment, and bundles of newspapers and magazines.

On the far side, away from the stairs, I saw the smoke. Above the smoke, light broke through the hole in the ceiling.

I moved forward and stopped immediately. I heard shuffling coming from behind a stack of papers blocking my view of the area. I knew that shuffling. Nothing sounds quite like a dead man walking, the unnatural dragging and stomping as one limb is pulled ahead to support the other.

I stood my ground as a zombie appeared around the corner, moving away from the area around the hole I'd yet to reach. He was a middle-aged man, bald, and wearing an apron from the local market. Smoke rose from his dead eyes as he stumbled through the darkness looking for a way out or something to eat.

He spotted me. I let him shamble towards me. From six feet away, I guessed I had thirty seconds to study him before he reached me. He was slower than slow. I looked at his eyes and saw the smoke swirling in and out of the space between eyeball and socket. It was as if the smoke caused both the death and the zombification. I'd never seen this. I was intrigued.

Unfortunately, baldy got too close, so I had to remove his cranium with the shotgun. His headless corpse fell within an inch of my shoe tips. The same green-tinted smoke rose from the bloody stump of his neck.

I stepped over the body and, as I reloaded, moved fast to the area below the hole in the ceiling.

There was a person there on the ground beneath the hole, an old woman with a white beehive hairdo. I saw now what had come through the house. It was a small glowing hunk of space rock, a meteor, I guessed. It was embedded in the woman's chest, and from the looks of her twisted limbs it had hit her in the bedroom and dragged her clear down to the cellar. She wasn't dead, but she should've been.

Though most of her old bones appeared shattered from the impact and fall, she still moved. Especially her head. It bobbed and writhed on mutated muscle and flesh. Her eyes were wide and green as fresh cut grass. Her mouth, gummy with clear slime, opened and closed like a hungry baby bird. She was fucking disgusting.

I kept my distance. I was reasonably sure this was where the outbreak began, but now I had a hunch there was more to it. Somehow the old lady drew living people to her and sent them away as flesh-eating zombies. And that rock melted into her guts had something to do with it, but how or why was anybody's guess.

So I decided to ask.

"You have two seconds to explain yourself," I said, "before I commence blowing your head all over the room."

The beehive bobbed and rolled. The neck was broken, but somebody forgot to tell the head.

After a second or two of drooling and slobbering (the old lady, not me), I lowered the shotgun at her head. There wasn't going to be any explaining. The thing on the ground was just a freak of nature, a radioactive, zombie-making, freak of nature.

Then...

"Wait..." the thing said. Its voice was garbled, slimy.

I kept the barrel on the head. "Speak."

"We... have... come... a... long... way." The thing spoke as its eyes rolled and smoke puffed from its mouth like a sickly tugboat.

The thing went on to explain, in a voice that sounded like a speaker drowned in a barrel of snot, that they were an alien race and a terrible disease had overtaken their planet, or some such shit, and here they were.

"Spreading the disease on our planet," I said. "Thanks a ton, asshole."

The beehive bobbled and garbled. If it was an apology, I didn't like it.

"So, where is this planet of yours?" I asked.

The arm of the spattered old lady rose out of the slime and rot like the limb of a mantis, and then dropped onto the meteor embedded in her gut. "Home... is here."

Wow. I stared at the writhing body and the rock, the planet in her gut. What an unbelievable turn of events; an entire planet falling to earth, hardly the size of a basketball. I'd seen some pretty amazing stuff in my time, but this took the cake. Absolutely astounding.

I almost felt bad when I blew its head all over the cellar.

As I exited the basement and removed the cloth from my face, I found out what the sound had been before. The old woman's yard was bustling with men in white bio-suits and soldiers in gas masks. In fact, they were everywhere. There were Jeeps and Hummers in the streets and helicopters in the air. Looked like the cavalry had finally arrived... too late, as usual.

I was immediately surrounded by soldiers with automatic weapons. They were all barking and yelling at me.

I just smiled. "You guys here to clean up my mess?"

Bang!

I was out cold. If I had to guess, I'd say it was a rifle butt.

When I came to I was in a small office. The walls were gray. So were the floors and ceiling. There was a small table and two chairs on either side. I sat in one. The other was empty. The floors, the whole room actually, hummed and vibrated. I realized then that it wasn't a room at all, but a mobile interrogation room. The military love their toys.

I wasn't tied up or handcuffed so I lit a smoke and waited for whoever I was waiting for to show up. I had my worries.

If the Feds had moved in for the clean up, anything was possible, depending on what they found, or thought they found. I didn't want to get mixed up in any Area 51 bullshit. I also didn't want Mo'Lock or any of his buddies getting pulled in for questioning. That could lead to big trouble.

About two and a half smokes after I came to, I had company join me in the mobile room. It was an older man, escorted by a couple guards. The older man wore a uniform, but I can never keep which one was which straight, so I'll guess and say he was Army, and from the amount of shit stuck all over his chest, I'd also guess pretty high ranking.

"Mr. McDonald, my name is General Theodore Adams."

"Hi, Ted," I replied.

He was not amused.

He dismissed the guards and sat in the opposite chair without offering to shake my hand. Fine. Fuck 'im.

The general narrowed his eyes at me. "How much do you know about what happened here today?"

"I know I stopped it."

He wasn't amused by that either.

"We have taken the 'object' from the basement and we have it contained," the general said.

I nodded. "Any survivors?"

"We found many of the town's residence hiding in their homes. We're estimating less than half of Mendez fell under the attack."

I pointed at him. "I suggest you destroy that 'object' before you have another outbreak."

"We'll take care of that. Don't worry, Mr. McDonald."

"So you know who I am?"

The general smiled and removed his hat. "My wife has a garden," he said. "She lives for that fucking thing. It makes her happy, but sometimes the garden gets bugs. Do you know what she has to do when she gets bugs?"

"Does she spray?"

"No," he went on. "She buys a predator bug and places it in the garden to go after and kill the harmful bugs."

I looked around. Was there a point to all this?

I shrugged.

The general pointed. "You're the predator bug," he said. "Near as we can tell you don't hurt anybody... except the bugs that hurt people, so we tolerate you."

"I'm a bug?"

I knew what he was saying. I didn't really give a shit and it didn't surprise me that they knew who I was. They'd have to be pretty stupid not to keep tabs on me. What I couldn't figure out was if they believed that there were monsters in the world. He seemed to imply they did, but they were fine letting me deal with it.

That made me mad. I was just one guy up against an entire subspecies, a separate populace who hunted humans, and this flippant attitude pissed me off. All I could think was that if I had the military on my side, the monster population of the world could be seriously damaged, if not wiped out entirely. I wondered if they realized how many murders around the world were committed by unnatural creatures.

The general leaned in. "Mr. McDonald, what I'm telling you is you're free to go."

I stood.

"But..."

I froze.

"...we'll be keeping an eye on you."

I shrugged. "Can I offer you a little advice?"

The general took a turn shrugging. "Sure."

"You may or may not believe in the things I know exist in the world," I said. "But that rock you pulled out of that old lady's gut is extremely dangerous. I think it would be in the world's best interest if you destroyed it instead of taking it away for study."

"I'll consider it."

"You should."

"I will."

"You'd better."

As confrontations go, it was pretty weak.

I walked out of the mobile interrogation room and into a military occupation of Mendez, California. The roads were blocked off, the dead were covered or gone, and everywhere I looked guys in uniforms were talking to survivors. I walked back the way I'd marched through town and found my Catalina parked where I left it.

My cell phone was lying on the seat with a note attached.

It read, "Cal. The Feds showed, so we left. Found your phone in a field. See you back in Los Angeles."

It was signed Mo'Lock.

I smiled. Who else gets shit on by humans and helped out by the dead? Just me. I started the car and left town thinking about the stupid story the general told me about the bugs and the garden. I guess it was a good analogy of what I do. I don't mind being a bug in the garden, I thought.

As long as I'm the bug doing the killing.


The End

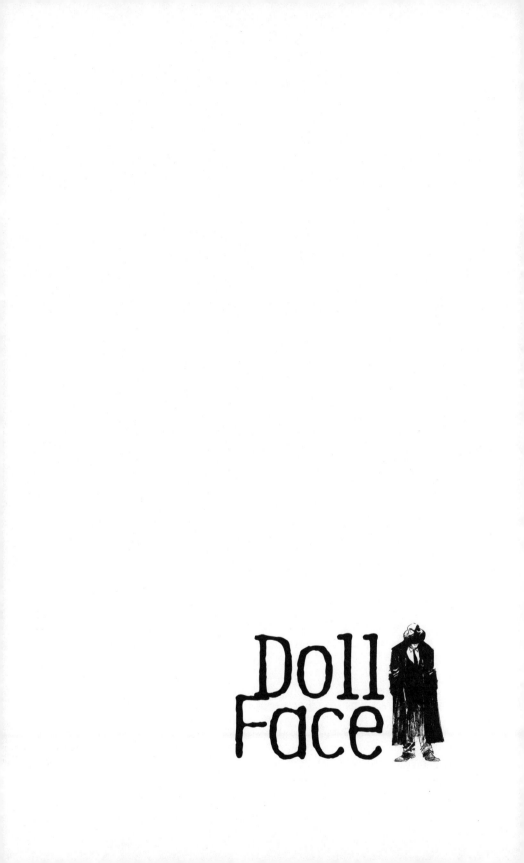

*Note: This story takes place before the bizarre events depicted in* Criminal Macabre.

# When I came to I was on

the floor of a jail cell. That in itself was bad enough, but I also had some company.

Some big fat fuck with thick glasses was trying to remove my belt. I didn't know if he was trying to steal or attempting some butt-pirating, and I didn't care. Using the flat of my palm I jammed his nose to one side, and then cracked it loose with the other.

I rolled to my feet and fat boy fell backwards against the

bars of the cell. I looked around quickly and saw three other cellmates staring, bored, like they'd seen it all before. I decided to give them something they'd never seen.

I finished removing the belt from my pants and pinned fat boy to the bars. I used the belt and tied him by his throat, then proceeded to wail on his chubby face until the guards showed up. I hadn't intended on it, but I must've tied the asshole to the door because when the guards pulled open the cell, fat boy got dragged along for the ride. My cellmates cracked up. So did the guards. Everybody was laughing except the asshole. He was unconscious.

When the laughing stopped and fat boy was peeled off the bars and taken away, one of the guards, a giant black guy with light eyes, looked at me and nodded. I nodded back. He was ghoul. A lot of LA cops are ghouls.

"Cal McDonald?"

"Yeah."

"Lieutenant Brueger wants to see you."

I waved goodbye to my cellmates and stepped around the half-circle smear of blood on the floor. I followed the big ghoul. I couldn't help but stare at him. He took up half the hall and almost reached the ceiling and those fucking eyes looked like they could shoot a laser beam.

"What's your name, Officer?" I asked. I think my staring was making him uncomfortable.

"Norris."

"Good to meet you, Norris," I said. "Any clue how I wound up here?"

"Disturbing the peace."

"Can you be a little more specific?"

"You threw a gentleman through the window of a sushi bar on Ventura Boulevard."

"Huh. No shit. I wonder why I did that?"

The ghoul cop grinned.

"While I'm asking stupid questions, who bailed me out?"

"I believe it was a young lady. A miss Sabrina Lynch."

"And she didn't stick around?"

The ghoul shook his head.

Shit.

This marked somewhere around the fifth time Sabrina had to bail me out of jail. She'd been nagging me about drinking, or more to the point, the things I did when I drank too much. I wasn't used to this relationship crap and I sure as hell wasn't used to anyone giving a flying shit about what I did or how much I did it.

Oh well, that was a shit-storm for later.

The ghoul stopped at the end of a long hall and pointed. "The Lieutenant's office is the first door on the right."

I stuck out my hand. "Good to meet you, Norris."

He shook my hand with his and my hand disappeared. "Good to meet you as well," he said, "and please tell Mo'Lock I said hello."

Before I could say anything he walked away. How the hell did Mo'Lock know him? Fucking ghouls networked better than Hollywood agents.

I walked to the first door. The door was old style with "Lieutenant Gretchen Brueger" painted in black on the fogged glass. I gave it three quick taps.

From the other side a female voice barked, "Come in!"

I pushed the door open and stepped inside.

I don't know what I expected, but the young, attractive woman sitting behind the desk was not it. The walls of the office were covered with framed awards and engraved plaques. There was even a key to the city from the mayor. You didn't have to be Einstein to figure out whoever this Lt. Brueger was, she had punched and crawled her way to the top of the LAPD.

She didn't know what the hell to make of me. She gave me a quick once over and then gestured for me to sit. She didn't offer me her hand.

"Cal McDonald," she said.

I nodded. I didn't say anything.

"So how long are you staying in Los Angeles?" she asked. Her tone dripped contempt.

"I moved here."

"I just read a four inch thick file on you," she raised one of her perfectly plucked eyebrows. "It looks like you spend a fair amount of time on both sides of the law."

"If that's what you want to call it."

She leaned forward. "You spent the night in a cell. What would you call it?"

"A black-out." I smiled.

She didn't.

There was a long, long silence. Almost too long. When I was about to leave, she cleared her throat. I stopped.

"I understand you claim to have dealt with... um... some unusual things in your life."

I nodded. "I deal almost exclusively with cases involving the so-called supernatural."

"So, you don't believe?"

"No, I just hate the word supernatural," I said. "It implies some sort of otherworldly hoodie-voodie and from my experience, the things I've confronted are very real, flesh and blood and all that crap."

She didn't want to come out with it and I wasn't about to make it easy. If she wanted to ask me about monsters, she was going to have to spit it out in plain English. I knew it was coming. It always did. These law enforcement types must run into more strange crap, but they always turn a blind eye. A man is found with giant holes in his neck and these pricks will call it a shooting. Who the hell shoots two perfectly placed shots into a guy's throat and with no exit wounds? That's what I call denial. It's like they refuse to accept how dangerous the world really is.

Finally she sat back in her chair and tried to smile. Maybe she was about to ask me what she wanted to ask, but I cut her off at the pass.

"How long have you been a cop?" I asked.

She seemed startled by the question. "Seems like my whole life," she said, almost to herself more than me. "I come from a family of cops."

"Are you the first to make Detective Lieutenant?"

"Um, no. I had a brother who made it. He was shot in the line of duty—"

"Sorry."

"—and my grandfather made Captain."

"So now that we got all of that out of the way," I smiled again. "How about you tell me why you called me in here. I'm guessing it's more than a shake-down."

Now she grinned. Not much of one, but it was there. "You're not what I expected."

"Oh yeah," I laughed. "What did you expect?"

"A drunken lout, I guess."

"Wait until tonight."

The air in the room was clear. She seemed relatively at ease. I didn't know it but in about two minutes I was the one who would be on edge.

"We have a suspect we're holding downstairs," she said. "I was wondering if you'd take a look at him for us."

I laughed. "Well, if you have a hold of him chances are he's not my kind of freak."

She stared at me. "He walked in here last night. He looked like, I don't know, an accountant or something; glasses, sweater vest, the type of guy you see a thousand times a day and never think twice."

I pretended to nod off.

"Except," she went on, "this guy walked into the station drenched with blood."

I opened my eyes. "Drenched?"

"Head to toe, like he'd swam in a vat of it."

"Okay, you got my attention," I said. "What else?"

"He refused to speak, or couldn't, but we arrested him and put him in a holding room for questioning. For five hours straight he just sat there and didn't make a sound, then all of a sudden he starts... I don't know how to describe it... babbling."

"Speaking in tongues maybe."

"Maybe." Brueger looked at me with an expression somewhere between lost and pissed off. I could see this guy had her good and freaked.

I asked her if they'd tested the blood. The tests came back as strange and inexplicable as the bloody man. It wasn't his blood. It was many people's blood all mixed together. She said the lab told her it would be impossible to separate the samples, but there could be as many as seventy-five to one hundred different possible blood samples in the mix.

"And he hasn't done anything but this babbling?" I asked.

"Pretty much, and it's constant, hour after hour."

I scratched my head. "You wouldn't happen to have a drink, would you?"

She glared at me.

"I didn't think so," I said. "Anything else?"

"Well, he did speak a couple words we could understand."

All I had to do was keep my mouth shut to avoid stepping in a big pile of shit. But it's amazing: sometimes the simplest things are the hardest to avoid.

"Yeah, what'd he say?" I said, walking right into it.

Brueger nodded. "He said your name."

Fuck.


I followed Brueger and a cop downstairs. I couldn't tell if the cop was a ghoul or not, but he sure as shit looked like one. But then again, most cops do. We took a back elevator from the bottom floor and went down one more. It looked like some kind of dungeon.

"What's with this place?"

The cop turned to me. He had huge wide set eyes and a nose like a boxer. "They used to bring perps down here in the old days, if you know what I mean."

I did. This was where they used to bring people to beat confessions out of them, and by the blood smudges on the walls and floor, the old days weren't so long ago.

Brueger tried to sanitize. "The new cells and interrogation rooms are in the next building. They're much nicer and modern."

The boxer-faced cop gave me a wink. I just looked back at him with a dull stare as we rounded a corner and came up on two cops standing outside one of the many doors lining the dingy hallway. One of the cops was Norris. He nodded when he saw me.

On the other side of the guarded door I could hear a muted voice. At first I thought it was two people talking at once, then as Norris cracked the door I realized it was one voice speaking at an impossibly fast speed. It sounded like an auctioneer on crack.

I glanced at Brueger. She stepped by me and pushed the door open all the way. Inside was a plain gray room with a table. There were two empty chairs and a small, skinny man sitting on the other side, handcuffed, his lips moving like a hummingbird's wings. His face was long and thin with a bizarre patch of hair right on top of his pointed head. He wore tan old man pants and a red short sleeve shirt. His arms were covered with either freckles or age spots.

He stared straight ahead at his own reflection in the two-way mirror. If he knew we were there, he gave no indication.

"That's all he does," Brueger said. "Any clue what the hell he's speaking?"

I listened to the furious babble of the skinny man for a second and then glanced at Norris. The language, if you want to call it that, reminded me of the speed-English ghouls spoke when they talked to each other. This was different. Brueger noticed me looking at the ghoul-cop. I quickly looked away. I knew how hard it was for the dead to blend with the living. I didn't want to blow his cover.

"Are you recording this?" I asked Brueger.

She nodded.

"Show me."

I followed Brueger to the room on the other side of the mirror. Inside a female officer, human, monitored the recording equipment set up on the table. Brueger introduced us quickly and then handed me off.

"You noticed the rhythm?" I asked.

The female cop nodded. "Yeah, whatever it is, he's saying it over and over."

"Have you tried playing it backwards?"

The female cop looked at me and turned as red as I've ever seen someone turn.

"No sir," she said.

I smiled. I wasn't trying to show her up. Sometimes the simplest fixes are the last ones you try.

After a couple clicks on her keyboard, the cop played a piece of the skinny man's babble backwards. The voice was strange, high-pitched, but it was English.

As we listened to the excerpt I stared at the suspect through the glass.

"...I killed them all and took their skin to my house on Moorpark right at the corner of Ponca. Tell me if you like what I did. I worked very hard..."

That was it. The same strange phrases over and over. Why he had blurted out my name was anybody's guess, but my guess was he was a fan. That's what I called the freaks who came after me since I'd become better known for doing what I do.

I had become so notorious for hunting monsters that every freak from Los Angeles to Romania thought they could take me out. They were wrong, of course, but it didn't keep them from constantly picking me as a target. Screw them. Screw all of them. Let them come. It's easier than tracking them down.

I drove to the corner of Moorpark and Ponca. It was located in a posh little pocket of homes near Warner Brothers Studios. Brueger wanted to come but I told her to stay and keep an eye on the skinny man. Instead, I dropped a line to my partner and creepy-ass ghoul, Mo'Lock. If things got weird, I wanted him around for backup.

There were four houses to choose from at that corner. Two had families I could see washing cars, playing in the yard and shit like that. The third was for sale and had an open house going. The fourth, a little Tudor-style number, had no activity, no car in the driveway and made my hair stand on end when I looked at it.

Mo'Lock arrived as I was heading across the Tudor's lawn. A cab dropped him off. The driver was also a ghoul. LA was worse than DC. Ghouls were fucking everywhere.

"What have we got?" he asked as I checked the front door for anything odd.

"Dunno," I said and kicked the door in. "Hey, look. It's open."

From the outside, the house looked pretty normal. The inside was the same except for some ugly-ass carpet. But there was a vibe hanging in the air like poison gas. There was something definitely wrong inside the skinny man's house. But did it have anything to do with bodies, like he said, or was it just a ruse to lure me in? Those were a couple of the thoughts racing through my mind.

In my pocket, my cell rang, and I jumped. Worse, the ghoul saw me and smiled. I glared at him and pointed. "Tell anyone and I'll bury you in ten feet of cement."

I answered. It was Brueger, checking on me.

"I'm in the house now," I said. "So far I don't see anything."

"I just wanted you to know," she said, "the suspect just stopped talking."

"What's he doing?"

"Just sitting and staring."

"Tell me if anything changes." I shoved the cell back in my pocket.

The ghoul had moved ahead of me into the living room, and he was so close to the wall it looked like he was sniffing the wallpaper. He ran his big, dead hands over the surface, slowly feeling for something, any kind of abnormality.

"You got something, Mo?"

"Possibly," he groaned. "There is a strange smell coming from behind this wall."

I walked over and joined in the wall-feel and I picked up slight traces of a sharp odor. It reminded me of shoe polish. As I ran my hands over a smooth spot, my fingers felt an inconsistency in the texture.

"Here." I said.

I gave the wall a push. There was a click and the panel opened. Classic hidden door bullshit. I glanced at Mo'Lock. He was looking at my hand on the wall.

"Cal... your hand."

There were spots on the back of my hand, freckles, like the skinny man's hands. A sinking nausea swelled in my throat and felt like a stone to my belly. Something had me. I didn't know what, but I knew, somehow. I also knew it was too late to do anything about it, so I pushed through the hidden door. The ghoul followed. I was pissed.

I should have waited. I should have taken a step back and looked at the situation, but I didn't and I walked right into the skinny man's trap. On the floor of the hidden room was a symbol like a pentagram, but more complex, with smaller signs inside each triangle. The pentagram was burned into the wood floor and I was inside it.

The ghoul had been smart enough to move slowly. He was outside the burned circle, looking around at the walls of the claustrophobic room. I looked up slowly and saw one of the worst sights I'd ever laid my eyes on.

The walls were covered with faces.

The skinny man had told the truth. He had taken his victims home. He'd skinned them and nailed their faces to the walls, their empty mouths stuck in permanent howls of pain, their eyes stretched wide and empty.

From the doorway I heard the ghoul. "You better get out of there, Cal."

But his warning was just for show. He had to warn me, but he knew by my expression I couldn't. He saw the spots growing on my now tightening skin.

I was stuck right where I stood. The symbol had me and held me in place with an invisible death grip and I was being drained of life.

I watched spots grow and spread up my arms. My skin turned sickly and transparent. Blue veins rose to the surface through the diminishing pigment. I could see small flecks of my flesh rising off me, like wisps of dandruff. They floated in the air around me, swirling, as if teasing me and then they whisked off, sucked into the eyes of the dead faces on the wall.

I didn't have a clue what to do and I was losing strength fast. I reached for the phone and dialed. Brueger picked up after half a ring.

"I was just calling you," she said. She sounded excited.

"Where's the—"

She cut me off.

"The suspect... he escaped."

I couldn't believe it.

"I don't fucking believe it! What happened? How?"

"H-he grew... or something, and snapped his cuffs," she said. "By the time anybody realized what was happening, he'd smashed the glass with the table."

I looked down. My body was shriveling.

"How did he get out of a police station?!"

I could hear her frustration. "I don't know," she said. "He just ran and before we knew it, he was gone."

"And he was bigger?"

There was a long pause. "Yeah."

"Is Norris there?" I asked. I needed a ghoul's perspective and help.

I waited.

"Norris here. What can I do for you, Mr. McDonald?"

"I know you can't talk in front of the humans, but I need you to spread word among the ghouls about this guy. I don't want him stopped or even touched."

At the door Mo'Lock looked as confused as Norris sounded.

I went on. "Just do it," I said. "If I know these bastards like I think I know them, he's heading straight over here to finish me off. Let him. It's the only chance I have."

Norris agreed. I hung up.

I could tell by the look on Mo'Lock's face I wasn't doing too well. I looked at my arms. I was so drained I could see my joints and my skin had begun to wrinkle and sag in between the gaps of bone. But what appeared to be aging, I feared, was much worse. My skin took on a gray hue and a smell rose from it like death. I wasn't aging, or just being drained. I was rotting away, right where I stood.

I didn't have to understand the exact hex to know I'd be dead in less than an hour if I didn't do anything, but I couldn't move my feet. It was like they were cemented to the floor.

"Mo'Lock," I barked. "Go into the garage and see it you can find me some kind of tool like a rake or a hoe!"

Mo'Lock nodded twice quickly and then ran back through the hidden door leaving me alone in the room with the circle and the faces. I was hardly aware of the flecks on my skin being pulled by a gentle current into the sockets and mouths. I scanned the faces, stretched and tacked, looking for anything common among them, but there was nothing. They were the faces of men and women and of varying races. The only thing they shared was a horrible death.

I twisted and turned, scanning the massive burned-in symbol that held me. It was a basic magic circle. Any asshole with a library card can learn how to make one, like a bomb from fertilizer or a nativity with Popsicle sticks. It was easy to obtain the info, but unlike those other items, a circle had to have a sequence of elements; the materials, the know-how and the will to bring it to life. Any one of those things could be the key, but figuring out which is like guessing which wire to cut on a bomb. Snip the wrong one and the whole thing could blow up in your face.

Only with this hoodie-voodie bullshit, you could wind up taking the whole fucking planet with you by unleashing God-knows-what.

Mo'Lock came running back to the room. If he breathed, he would have been breathing hard. His deep sunken eyes were wide and wild. In his arms he had a rake, an axe, a hoe and a Weed Whacker with the long orange cord dangling behind.

"Don't break the circle," I said, "Just place them down where you are."

Mo'Lock placed the lawn tools down on the floor where I could reach them, then he looked up at me.

"He's coming."

I knew who he meant, but I asked anyway.

The ghoul nodded. "He's walking down the street calm as can be, with police trailing right behind him," he said. "And he's big... very big."

"Great."

I looked at the tools and began to reach for the hoe, but then the Weed Whacker caught my eye. I grabbed it and chucked the cord to the ghoul. He plugged it in.

"Are you sure this is wise?" Mo'Lock said. "I suspect it will take more than that to stop this gentleman."

I grinned. My face felt tight and bony. I was glad I couldn't see myself.

"This isn't for him," I said.

By the looks of my hands holding the bright orange grass cutter, I could see I was little more than a skeleton with a thin layer of transparent veiny flesh holding me together. Even the lightweight tool felt heavy in my hands.

By now I could hear a ruckus outside. I heard sirens and voices speaking through bullhorns telling the suspect to stop. I could tell by the repeated order he wasn't listening.

I revved up the Whacker and it sputtered. I yelled for the ghoul to clear the room and to stay out of the skinny man's way. I wanted him to come after me. I wanted him to break the circle, and I was pretty sure when he saw my indoor gardening he'd do it.

The Whacker purring in my hands, I began running the business end over dead faces nailed to the wall. If that was the conduit of my flesh, then I had to destroy them. As the spinning cord touched the first face, an empty-eyed male with a mustache, the flesh blew apart like gelatin and made a sickening sound as chunks of face began to fly from the wall.

I swept the wall with the Whacker and soon it was raining fleshy debris. Outside I heard slamming and banging as the skinny man made his way into the house. He was yelling my name. There was anger and panic in his voice. I knew I was on the right track. I'd disturbed the hex.

I quickly worked my way around the walls of the confined room, slashing and mowing the faces of the skinny man's victims. Chunks and dust flew, blinding me as I saw a shape appear in the doorway. It was the skinny man, but he wasn't skinny anymore. He filled the doorway with his new stolen body.

When he saw what I was doing he charged at me. I was defenseless except for the Weed Whacker so I spun at my hips and connected with the side of his face as he barreled in. His face tore open and howled. He also broke the circle. My feet snapped free and I fell backwards against the wall with only the lawn tool between my withered body and the skinny man.

"You think you're so fucking great!" he yelled.

I had no idea what he was talking about.

I clocked him right across his nose with the whirling plastic blade and split his face open. He grabbed at his face, but it was too late. The dried flesh flecks clouding the room began to stick to the wound, and soon the gash was a vacuum sucking in the dust.

I could feel my strength returning, but not fast enough. The killer let go of his face and grabbed me by my jacket. He lifted me off the ground and pounded me back and forth against one wall, then the other. I tried to hit him with the blade again. I was too close. He yanked it from my hands and smashed it onto the floor.

I tried my best to resist, to get a few choice punches in, but I was still weak. On his face the two gashes I'd made were bloated with murdered flesh particles crawling inside the killer's body. I planted my palm into the bridge of his nose and made another bloody opening. The particles leapt from the air into his face, attacking the opening.

My strength was returning, and the skinny man was shrinking. I saw fear in his eyes. I saw him for the coward he was and he knew it. He let me go and tried to back away, swiping at his face like a man attacked by a swarm of bees. But these weren't insects. He was under attack by the fragmented spirits of those he'd murdered to create destructive black magic.

I stood and balled my fist. I was almost back to normal. I walked towards him and laid one right on the side of his face, leaning in with all my returning weight. I connected and the skinny man spun. Blood sprayed the wall. I kneed him in the groin. When he buckled I used the other knee to his face and stood him upright again.

One last ball of knuckles knocked him out.

I stood over the skinny man as the particles invaded his body, a last desperate attempt to have revenge on their killer.

By the time Brueger and her buddies stormed in yelling cop warnings, it was over. The dust had settled.


Later, after the skinny man was dragged away, he was identified as Karl Doll, a single accountant for one of the studios. In one of the rooms we found a box of news clippings. They were all about me. Evidently Karl fancied himself a junior monster hunter but he was jealous of me and thought if he could take my energy, he could do what I do.

Fuck that wimp. If you can't do it with what you have, you can't do it.

Thinking about what he did, killing people to get something from me, made me glad I didn't kill him like I wanted to. Let him go to trial and look at the faces of the families of those poor people he killed. Let him go to jail. With any luck he'd wind up in a cell with a belt thief, the way I was.

The whole horrible thing showed me just how vulnerable I had made myself allowing magazines like the *Speculator* write about me.

Then it hit me.

I'd never called Sabrina. As far as she knew she'd bailed me out of jail and then I'd blown her off. There would be no sweet talking my way out of this one.

Fuck.

From one shit-storm to the next.

The End

# Tuesday, the fifth of

September, began like any
other day; I woke up, threw
up, and went back to bed. It
was five-thirty in the evening.
Cases were few. I was, and
had been, completely flat
fucking broke the better
part of a long and shitty L.A.
summer.

By the time I got showered and dressed it was almost six-thirty and dark. There was a hot, dry breeze blowing through the house. Within seconds of getting out of the shower my skin dried up and scabs were falling off me like dead flies. I'd had a run-in with a gang of fiends a few days before. Those fucks have some nasty unkempt fingernails and they scratched the crap out of me. I beat their skulls in with a hammer.

To help get the blood flowing, I swigged down some coffee spiked with whiskey. A Vicodin chaser would help me to achieve the proper balance for the night. Unfortunately, the only bottle I had was as empty as my wallet. I had to down the pill dry.

The phone rang as I began to gather all my empty liquor bottles—about thirty in  all. I was interrupted, of course.

"Yeah?"

"It's me." The voice sounded like dry bones. Fucking ghoul.

"Mo'Lock, what the hell are you doing? Where are you?"

He took a deep, slow breath. "I am right outside," he groaned, "I just walked from Ventura Boulevard. There is an interesting street fair happening and—"

"Quit fucking around. Get your dead butt in here." I spat, and slammed the receiver down.

While I waited for the ghoul I began turning the bottles upside down in glasses around my office/house. Well, technically it was my old friend Sam Burnett's house, but since the whole "losing his head" incident, he left it to me and left the country. I think getting duped by a teenage burnout really took it out of the old guy.

The bottom of a dirty glass was filling drop by drop with alcohol, but I'd get a fucking shot one way or another. Just as I turned over the fifteenth bottle, Mo'Lock came lumbering in looking pale and disoriented, which was fine 'cause that's how he always looks. He's a ghoul after all. They're not known for their color or grace. Lumbering's about as good as it gets.

"Hey," I said, continuing to turn the bottles.

"Hello," said Mo'lock, and he crossed the room to the window behind my desk. "What are you doing?"

"Trying to get a drink," I said. "Where you been? Ain't seen you in weeks."

He looked out the window and said, "I fell asleep."

I nodded, telling myself not to ask. I'd only get more confused. Ghouls sleep? You learn something new every fucking day, I guess.

Finally I got to the last bottle and I was pleased to see I had more than a shot. I took the glass and kicked bottles aside as I went to my desk.

Mo'Lock turned his head. "Any cases?"

"Zero, zilch, not-a-one."

"Broke?"

"Completely." I sipped my whiskey. Ahhh.

The ghoul made a noise similar to a cat sneeze and said. "If you want I could loan you some money."

I choked a little. "What the f—"

Before I could finish he had produced a wad of cash you could kill a man with. And from where I was sitting I could see that it was all in twenties and hundreds.

I swigged the last drops from the glass and stood. "Where the hell did you get that?!" I yelled.

"From my fellow ghouls," he droned. "All monies made by ghouls are thrown into a collective slush fund for everybody to enjoy."

"What are you, dead or a hippie?!"

"What is a hippie?"

I waved him off. "Never mind." I rubbed my eyes. "I don't mean no disrespect, but what the fuck do you need money for?"

"Cabs."

I held back my laughter. "Could you loan me a few bucks so... I... ah... can get a few things?"

There was a short pause. "Sure, here's forty."

"Thanks," I said laughing a bit as I took the bills from his big white hand. "You suppose you could watch over the place while I pop to the store for a few necessities?"

He agreed. I put on a jacket and grabbed a baseball cap I'd grown out of about ten years ago. But I liked it, so I stuck it on the back of my head and left the office.

I walked out the door of my house, and as if on cue, it started raining. Just a drizzle, but enough to piss me off, and it was that shitty LA rain. Hot and wet. It might sound good in a porno movie, but in real life it sucked ass.

I walked fast down Laurel Canyon to Ventura and as I moved closer to the liquor store I saw a guy leaning against a wall ahead of me. I could see he was trouble. Long, lanky and greasy, he wore a wide smirk on his face as he watched me approach. At first I thought he might have been a ghoul, maybe a fiend, or even a goon, but as I got closer I saw he was just human.

When I was within several feet of him, he looked right at me and his smirk widened. "Nice hat," he said.

I smashed my fist across the side of his nose and felt it snap beneath my knuckles. "Nice nose," I said, and kept going without losing a step. Fucking loser.

As much I wanted to, I didn't look back, but I could hear the guy "oh-my-godding," and "jesus-christing." I felt pretty good. Might be a good night after all.

I bought a big, jug-sized bottle of whiskey, a case of good cheap beer and a carton of cigarettes. I had enough left over so I grabbed a lighter and a large bag of chips for dinner.

I was disappointed to see that Mr. Smart-mouth was gone but there was a decent puddle of blood and a trail of drops that led across the street. They were big and wide apart so I knew the guy had run like a sissy. I laughed a little and headed back to the pad, not minding the steaming drizzle a bit.

I was already on the porch of the house when I heard muttering voices coming from inside. They didn't sound threatening, but just to be sure I slowly placed my armload down next to the door and drew my gun.

There were two voices. One kept interrupting the other and both spoke quickly. Then when I heard what I thought was Mo'Lock's voice, I eased the door open with my left hand and fixed the gun, cocked, in my right. The door clicked and slid. Inside the office all eyes turned on me. Three sets of 'em.

Mo'Lock was sitting at my desk, his feet up, entertaining two suits. I put my gun away, glancing at the two assholes, then slowly up at the ghoul, nodding my head. "What's goin' on here?" I said.

Mo'Lock took his feet down. "I was just briefing these two potential clients—"

I shook my head.

Mo'Lock stood and walked away. "Damn."

I grabbed the packages, dragged them inside the door, and slammed it shut. Then I eyeballed the two geeks in suits. I saw that one of them had a ponytail. I hate that shit. We were off to a bad start, I thought as I snagged a beer, then went around the back of my desk and sat.

I was right on one count. These two were major geekoids. The one on the right, Mr. Fuckin' ponytail, had on the fattest, ugliest tie in the universe and it was stained with all manner of scum. The suit itself was the color of vomit after a frozen dinner, and believe me, I know that color. His face was that of a true dullard; long and thin with half-closed eyes and a slobbery hanging lower lip.

Basically he looked like a half-hearted hippie in a bad suit. I wanted to point out what a hippie looked like to the ghoul, but I let it ride instead of immediately alienating some potential cash.

The other guy was different, but a geek just the same. He had on a black suit, bowtie, white socks and brown shoes. He had thin greasy black hair, big-ass horn-rimmed glasses and a face that only a mother could love, if she were blind and retarded.

They both screamed to be beaten up.

"So, gentlemen—" I belched. "What can I do for you today?"

The guy with the glasses got nervous and sat forward pushing back his glasses with his finger. "Um, ah, my name

is Sinclair Walters, Mr. McDonald, and this is my partner, Alex Daniels," he said, gesturing to the ponytail.

"How nice. What d'you want?" I said as I swigged my beer and glanced over at Mo'Lock.

"I... I mean we... are—" Horn-rimmed stuttered.

Ponytail Daniels broke in with a cocky snort. "What Dr. Walters is trying to say, is that we need to ask you for a favor, Mr. McDonald."

"I don't do favors."

Ponytail rolled his eyes in a way that told me this kid was used to getting his way, which really pissed me off. A geek is one thing, but a pushy geek demanded a severe beating. I was about to inform him of this when he broke in.

"Maybe we should start with a question," he said, "Do you believe in the soul, Mr. McDonald?"

I slammed down my beer can. "What kind of goddamn question is that?! Do I believe in souls?"

I acted extra angry to watch them jump. Mo'Lock tried his best not to smile.

Horn-rimmed was sweating like a dorky pig and I could see Mr. Ponytail was getting annoyed. Good. Fuck 'em. Then he took a breath.

"It's a fairly basic question. Do you believe in the human soul?"

I shrugged. "I believe in filet of sole, soul food, and I believe that the sole of my boot is about to become the biggest fucking suppository in the world if you don't get to the goddamn point," I said, and stood.

They were stunned, so I used the time to throw Mo'Lock a wink and grab the bottle from the bag. By the time

I swigged a few and returned to my desk the schmuck brothers were ready to talk biz.

Horn-rimmed talked first. "We've heard about you for a long time, read about your exploits in *Speculator Magazine*, and we know that you have a sort of expertise in a particular area of work. We know that you have had encounters with... eh...."

"A lot of weird shit," I cut in.

Ponytail nodded and took over. "We are in the process of some very 'weird' research, Mr. McDonald, and we would like to hire you to act as an adviser."

I looked over at Mo'Lock, then back to the boys. "What exactly are you guys doing? What sort of 'research'?"

They looked at each other. Ponytail nodded as if telling Horn-rimmed that it was okay to tell.

Horn-rimmed looked at me sheepishly. "I'll have to ask you one more time, Mr. McDonald. Do you believe in the soul?"

I groaned. "God almighty. If it'll get you to the fucking point, yes, I believe, I believe!" I moaned.

To my side Mo'Lock giggled. It wasn't some girlish giggle, but a raspy dead man's convulsion.

Ponytail seemed relieved by my sudden surge of belief and dropped the bomb. "My partner and I have devised a method by which we can capture the essence of a human being, the soul."

Mo'Lock stepped over to the desk. "What do you mean when you say capture?" he said.

The ghoul sounded suddenly on edge. I raised my hand. He nodded and went back to the window.

Horn-rimmed took over. "Not really capture, but we believe we can bring a human soul into the physical world."

I swigged out of the bottle, nodding, and then I threw my hands up. "So, the million dollar question stands. What the hell do you need me for?"

"We just need you to be there with us during the procedure." Said Ponytail.

I looked at Mo'Lock, then back at them. "What, as a fuckin' good luck charm, a goddamn cheerleader?!"

Horn-rimmed pushed back his rims. "Well... yes, in a sense."

I thought about it.

"What's the pay?"

"A thousand for the day. In advance."

"Whoa, for that I'll bring my pom-poms."

Everyone nodded and smiled. That is, except for Mo'Lock. He seemed none too pleased about the whole deal, but he knew enough not to say anything in front of the clients. He knew I needed that grand bad, so he just stood at the window while I made all the arrangements. The big day was set for the day after tomorrow at a warehouse in South Central LA. They gave me the cash and that was that.

Mo'Lock was quiet for awhile. I ignored him and concentrated on my drinking. He stood at the window, sighing heavily every minute or so, trying to get me to ask him what was wrong, but I wasn't gonna. No way. If the fuckin' ghoul had something to say, come out and say it. I don't play counselor. Besides, it was fun watching him pout.

After about an hour of hearing the ghoul breathe like a bulldog I was drunk and sick of the game. I slammed down the half-empty bottle of whiskey. "Okay, okay. What the hell's wrong, Mo'? I give up. Tell me what's wrong."

Mo'Lock turned to me slowly like he was trying to play up the drama. "If they can do what they say they can do, the ramifications could be disastrous."

"Ramifications?! Hoo, boy! You been reading the dictionary, dead-boy, or what?"

"Cal, I'm serious."

I nodded. He was serious. I curbed my dickheadedness. "Okay, but let's say they can't do what they say. That's what I think's most likely the case. I think I'm gonna pull a cool grand watching these jerks toot their horn."

"But what if they can?

I shrugged. "What real harm could it do?"

Mo'Lock started to say something, but stopped himself and just shook his head turning back to his window. I waited and watched him. Nothing.

Then he turned to me. "They're messing with dangerous territory, even if they don't get results this time," he said.

I wanted to agree, I did agree, but all I could see was a thousand bucks. "Well, that's the chance I'm gonna have to take," I said. "It has nothing to do with you. Besides, I've dealt with weirder shit before. Don't worry."

The ghoul turned back to the window. "You've never had your soul taken from you, have you, Cal?" he asked, and that was all that was said for the rest of the evening.

The day arrived as most do with me: late and in a pool of vomit. I'd passed out at my desk the night before after being thrown out of a few bars, kicked around by some cops and generally harassed by the planet. I felt like shit and was in no mood to deal with those science geeks, let alone their lame-o experiment.

I wiped the vomit off my desk and was surprised to see I'd had a pretty decent dinner. Looked like steak. Too bad I couldn't remember.

I took a big swig as I glanced at the clock. It was almost five. I had an hour to get my shit together and get over there. I didn't have time to waste so I took the bottle with me and got into the shower. I killed the bottle, washed, hocked up some bile and before I knew it I felt like I might not kill somebody.

Mo'Lock was waiting for me outside the house. I had gotten the idea that he wasn't tagging along so I figured he was just gonna give me a hard time. "Hey, gruesome, you coming?"

He nodded. "What else have I got to do," he said. "Besides, knowing you, there's bound to be trouble."

I laughed. "Let's hope you're wrong," I said as I got into my car.

We pulled up in front of a big gray warehouse just as the sun set. I got out and lit a smoke, surveying the big building hidden in the shadow of some other abandoned houses. The warehouse was half stone and half steel. The kind they use for airport hangars and army barracks. Very dull, very cold and so plain I doubted I would have ever seen it if I hadn't been looking for it.

There was a single door stuck on its front like a pig snout. No windows, just a few vent ribbings above the doorway where the stone turned to steel. Next to the door there was an unmarked buzzer button. I pressed it as Mo'Lock came up behind me.

I turned to him. "Look, about the other night..." I began.

Mo'Lock shook his head. "Do not worry about it. Let's just get this over with."

I was about to tell him again that I doubted the experiment would even work when the door opened and there peeking around the corner was Ponytail. He was wearing a lab coat.

"You're late," he said.

We pushed passed him. "Yeah, I know," I said. "So let's get to it."

Ponytail led us along a dark white stone corridor for what seemed like the length of the warehouse, then turned and took us another twenty feet to a double steel door. I looked around. The door, as well as the stone walls, were new. It looked like the junior science corps had done some expensive renovating.

Outside the door was a combo-lock. Ponytail slid a card through a slot, then punched some numbers on a tiny keyboard. There was a buzz, a beep and then finally a click followed by the hiss of the door pushing open. He signaled for us to follow, which we did.

Inside was something out of either a really cheap or really expensive science fiction movie. I couldn't decide. The room was huge and had a massively high ceiling. Everywhere you looked lights were flashing, machines beeped, liquid ran through tubes and computers cranked. They even had one of those arc-light deals buzzing above a huge glass tank in the center of the room.

Inside the tank was a slab, and on the slab was a naked man hooked to wires from every part of his body. A machine outside the tank beeped along, telling us he was alive. And as if that wasn't enough, pointing at the tank was a syringe the size of a Chevy. Its huge needle, a fuckin' tube really, stuck into the tank.

Even Mo'Lock was impressed. I looked over at him and we both did that wide-eyed thing.

Ponytail was nodding his head beside me waiting for me to ooh and ahh. "Well, what do you think?"

I bobbed my head. "Quite a chemistry set you got here, kid. Where do you want us?"

"Over there," he said, pointing to a couple of chairs to the left of the tank.

As he said this, Horn-rimmed came in from another door and jumped when he saw us. Skittish fuck.

I ignored him and we went over to the chair and sat. "You boys run along and do your thing. I'll be over here cheering," I said, and sat.

Mo'Lock sat down next to me and crossed his big legs. As I took out my flask, he leaned over to me and whispered, "Creepy, isn't it?"

I took a swig, offered some to the ghoul. He shook his head. "Fucking stupid, if you ask me."

For the next hour we watched the two geeks scramble around the room pushing this, turning that and being science types. For all I knew they were doing nothing. It was all a bunch of knobs and tubes to me. I was getting pissed because I'd emptied the flask in the first fifteen minutes.

At one point Horn-rimmed got close to us. I belched really loud and he jumped. "Hey Einstein," I said pointing to the tank, "Who's the stiff?"

"Oh, ahh, that... that is... ahhh, Mr. Andrew Thomas Blue," he blubbered.

I nodded. "And what's his deal?"

Horn-rimmed pushed his glasses back. "Well, he uh, has been kept alive by machines for a year now and... well, his family finally signed the papers to have him cut off."

I looked at Mo', then laughed, looking back at the geek. "Bet they didn't know he'd wind up in Frankenstein's lab, did they?"

"Well, ahh... no. We had to shuffle a few papers."

"I bet you did."

Finally they were ready. Horn-rimmed sat at a panel behind the tank while Ponytail took position at the machine attached to Mr. Blue.

"Hey Doctor, where's the popcorn?" I shouted.

Ponytail turned and shushed me. "Mr. McDonald, please. You are being paid well."

He had me there. I shut my trap. They began working feverishly. Ponytail had one hand on what I assumed was the cut-off button and one finger in the air that Horn-rimmed was staring at. Slowly Ponytail turned a switch and then signaled his partner by lowering his finger.

"Now," he whispered.

Suddenly the tank was filling with a smoky blue mist that came from the giant syringe. It filled quickly and as it did Ponytail completed turning off his machine and backed away, staring intensely into the mist.

I realized that both Mo'Lock and I were standing and staring too. At first I couldn't see a thing, but then gradually something began to form in the thick mist above the body inside. I moved closer.

There was something solid in there but I couldn't make it out. The shifting mist made it hard to see what was going on inside the tank.

Then Ponytail signaled Horn-rimmed again and the syringe began sucking out the smoke. It was gone in seconds.

Behind me I heard the ghoul let out a gasp.

They'd done it. I was stunned.

There, floating above the body was another body, naked and as blue as a summer sky. It floated, facing the corpse as though studying it. It was the dead man's soul. A motherfucking human soul. I couldn't believe it, but there it was. It was odd it didn't really look like the dead man. The corpse was old and flabby, but the spirit was smooth and muscular, almost featureless. It was staring at the corpse below it.

Then slowly it began to rise away from the corpse and was only a few feet short of the top of the tank.

Everybody was standing around the tank, silent, in awe. I hate to say shit like this, but it was as if we were all sharing the same dream. We just watched the soul rise, floating as gentle as a feather.

Then it hit the top of the tank.

The spirit jolted and bumped the top. It shook, it spun, it shuddered and suddenly the blue mist form began to take on a greasy, solid form. It tried to rise again, but nothing, it hit the roof again. For a moment it just stayed there, suspended. Then it seemed to decide something and began to descend to the body again. It was trying to get out, but it would find no way there either.

The spirit just bumped against the body as it had the roof. Then it began to panic. It began flying around the tank, trying every direction. It hit the glass and the sound of it made us all jump.

Mo'Lock stepped toward it. "It's trying to get out."

But no one said a word. We just watched the soul swim in its cage. The expression on its smooth blue face was one

of agony, fear, confusion. I suddenly felt terrible. This is what Mo'Lock had been afraid of. I understood. Souls are supposed to pass on to some other place or form, not get trapped in a big fish tank.

I looked over at Ponytail. He was grinning at me. "Well, Mr. McDonald. Do you believe in souls now?"

I glared at him. I almost attacked him, but where the fuck would that get me? I walked toward the door instead and signaled the ghoul to follow.

As we passed by Ponytail I shot him one last glare. "You suck," I said and left.

Behind me I could hear the soul pounding against the glass.


Back at my office I got good and drunk but it didn't help. I felt like shit. I couldn't believe I was a part of that horror. Mo'Lock was standing at the window staring out and didn't say a word for hours.

Then... "It's not your fault, Cal," he said. "You didn't know."

I looked at him. I was slobbering drunk and could hardly speak. "You told me. I didn't listen."

"Now you know."

I shrugged a drunken shrug. "Shit."

I was about to whine some more when there was a crash outside in the yard. I sprang to my feet and pulled my gun. I was drunk but not that drunk. Mo'Lock came over to me as I came around the desk. There was another crash, then a thud and with each noise whatever was out there got closer to my door. Then it hit the door. The ghoul stepped over to it while I fixed my gun on it.

I nodded. He opened the door.

There at the door was Horn-rimmed, sans specs. He was covered with blood, beaten to a pulp, his lab coat torn apart. The top right side of his head had been chopped away and I could see skull and brains. The kid should have been dead.

He had time to say two words: "Mr. Blue." Then he fell, smashing his skull completely open on the floor.

I stared down at the brains.

I looked at Mo'Lock. "Shit," I said.

The ghoul nodded slowly. "Shit indeed."

I shook my head, then walked over to the doorway and helped Mo' drag the body inside so we could shut the door. I knew what was coming and I didn't like it a bit.

Mo'Lock beat me to the punch. "We better get over there."

This time I did the nodding.

We got to the warehouse a little after one in the morning. The front door was ajar as we walked up to it. All was quiet. I had my gun drawn. We made our way inside. The corridor was dark. The walls and floor were smeared and spattered with blood. We moved along taking quiet steps and avoiding the blood.

At the end of the hall we peeked around the corner. There was light coming from where the double steel doors had been. They had been ripped out of the wall.

I listened. Nothing. Then suddenly a noise like shifting feet. I edged around the corner, my gun out in front. Then I stopped. Inside someone spoke.

"I hear you out there." It was a woman's voice. "You can't hide. Get in here," she said.

I looked at Mo'Lock. He shrugged. I bobbed my head and we turned the corner.

The lab was painted red with blood. Everything in the place was destroyed. There was a woman there, bright blue and naked. She was changing even as we stepped through the door, changing into something else, a man, a child. I couldn't tell. It was as if it was trying to figure out what it was.

Then finally it settled on the form I'd seen in the tank and it stood there looking at us. At its feet was a corpse I could only guess had been Ponytail. The Blueman had ripped his flesh completely from his body. All that was left was a skeleton covered with glistening fat and muscle tissue.

His skin was lying in a pile nearby like a wad of dirty laundry.

The soul took a step toward us. "You were part of this. You took me away," it said angrily, and then just as fast, slumped sadly. "Now I'll never know where I was going."

I pointed at the pile of skin on the floor. "I'd say after this the answer's pretty clear."

I immediately regretted saying anything.

The soul came right at me. It was mad. It shape-shifted as it took strides towards me, each step triggering a new form. Man, woman, child, big, small, short. All blue, all mad, and all coming right at me. I fired the gun but it had no effect. The bullets didn't bounce. The soul just absorbed them.

I tried to jump out of its way but it got a grip on me and the next thing I knew I was flying through the air. I hit the wall. I felt ribs snap. I looked up.

Mo'Lock was going after the thing, but it wouldn't fight him. It just kept coming after me. The ghoul grabbed onto it and tried to stop it and the thing lashed out and turned to him.

"I have no quarrel with you. You are soulless. Get off me!" it screamed, and threw the ghoul clear to the other side of the room.

It swung at me. I dodged and leapt out of the way, just missing a fist that smashed stone. But it kept after me. I saw it coming, still shifting and this time it was getting bigger and bigger until it had turned into the biggest fucker I had ever seen in my life.

I was frozen.

It lifted me off the floor and pulled me close to its face.

"Do you have any more wisecracks before I kill you?! Any last words?! Do you?! DO YOU?!" it screamed.

I was done for. I looked him right in the face. His hot odd breath went right up my nostrils. "You know, dead or not, a Tic-Tac would go a long way," I said.

BAM!

It felt like a bowling ball smashed against my head and I was flying through the air again. My nose was definitely broken, maybe my jaw, maybe my entire head was broken.

I hit the floor, moaned and rolled. But the damn thing had me by my legs and was spinning me. I started barfing and all I could think was poor Mo'Lock, having to get sprayed by my puke.

Then it got worse. The blue soul-thing let me go. Wheee! I was beyond pain. I was a meat-bag flying through the air.

I hit brick, wood, plastic and finally glass. I was pulp. And it was still after me. I could see it through bloodied eyes. I was doomed.

But Mo'Lock was there too. I'd forgotten. He was running to get in between me and the beast, but Mr. Blue just kept coming at me. There was nothing I could do. I couldn't even feel my arms or legs, let alone move.

Mo'Lock didn't fight. He didn't even raise a fist. The ghoul did the one thing I didn't expect.

He inhaled.

He faced the blue beast and sucked in a lungful. The soul stopped in its tracks. Mo'Lock sucked again and this time I swear to God the side of the blueman's face was pulled outward toward the ghoul. He sucked again, and harder, and suddenly the entire side of the monster was being stretched, sucked toward Mo'Lock.

Now Mr. Blueman was the one screaming. It was trying to get away, but old Mo' just kept sucking and sucking, breathing in and out as hard as he could get his dead lungs pumping, until he was at last actually drawing the flesh of the blue man into his mouth. Sucking and sucking and sucking.

It was unbelievable. I got to my feet, dripping blood, and watched awestruck as inch by inch, Mr. Blue disappeared into the ghoul. And after a minute it was done. No more Mr. Blueman. It was just me and the ghoul.

I shook my head and stepped over to him. I think everything was broken, but I was too happy and stunned to pay attention. "Are there any other things you can do you'd like to tell me about?" I laughed.

Mo'Lock seemed disoriented. He turned like he was lost and then looked at me with utter surprise. "Where am I?" he asked.

I laughed. "You're here... in the lab... with me. Hey, Mo'Lock, you okay?"

The ghoul's face twisted. "And who are you, sir?" he said, and it wasn't Mo'Lock's voice. It was higher pitched, and kind of snooty.

"It's me, Cal. What's the matter Mo'Lock?" I said.

I reached out for his arm.

He jerked it away. "Unhand me! And what is this Mo'Lock? My name is Michael Thomas Locke! And I want you to tell me where I am. And where are my wife and children?"

Oh God, no.

"Don't you know who I am, Mo'?"

"No, I should say not."

I felt a ball growing in my throat as I began to understand what was happening. "What year is it, Mr. Locke?" I asked, barely whispering.

He was indignant. "What kind of question is that? It's 1919!"

I walked away. I didn't know what else to do. I thought about shooting him, maybe freeing the soul from his body, but what if it just killed him? I couldn't take that chance.

Behind me, Michael Thomas Locke was yelling. I didn't listen. I didn't care. Mo'Lock was gone. He got a soul back and now he was his former self again. I walked out of the place and tears kept coming.

What'd he have to go and do a thing like that for? Crazy fucking ghoul.

To save my lame-ass life, that's why.

I didn't go to the hospital. Fuck that. I went back to the house and drank until I could barely see, let alone stand or speak. I tried not to think about Mo'Lock, and the fact that he was gone forever. Christ, he was a fuckin' ghoul, a spook. I'm supposed to be killing them. Not forming close personal bonds, right? I mean, he wasn't even human. Well, now he was. I wondered if he liked it.

The night passed and before I knew it I was waking up slumped over my desk. The sun was blaring in through the cracks in the blinds. My head pounded as I looked around the room and for the first time in my life a feeling hit me. I felt alone and somehow that was worse than my injuries and the hangover combined.

I swigged from my whiskey until it overflowed from the corners of my mouth, until my mind and body numbed, but the feeling stayed. The phone rang. I ignored it. Whoever it was could go fuck themselves.

Then there were footsteps outside. It was the landlord, most likely. I dug into the top drawer of the desk and pulled out a wad of bills and stood. When he came through the door I was going to throw the bills into his face. Maybe that would feel good. The steps stopped outside the door and there was a quiet rapping.

"Come in," I said

The door opened. I dropped the bills.

It was Mo'Lock.

I squinted. "Mo'? Is that you?"

The ghoul stepped in, nodding. "Yes, it's me."

I could have hugged the big dead freak. I didn't though. I just stood there looking stupid. "What happened to Mr. Blue?"

Mo'Lock shrugged. "I let him go." He said and smiled. "I didn't like being me again."

Now I smiled. "You were kind of uptight. You didn't like me, that's for sure," I said.

I looked down at myself and realized I was covered with blood.

Mo'Lock put his hand on my shoulder and began pulling me out the door. "You look like you could use a few thousand stitches. Let's get you to the hospital."

I followed the ghoul out of the house and to my car. "Don't read into this too much," I said, "but I'm glad you came back."

"Me too," he said. "Besides, you owe me forty bucks."

## The End

Stitch

# Have you ever had déjà vu

and then realized that your life was repeating itself, that the same horrible things kept happening over, and over, and over? If you have, then you might have some small smidge of an idea what it's like to be me.

My name is Cal McDonald. I hunt monsters. If you wanted to be all dramatic and shit, you could say that monsters are my business.

I was visiting the hospital to have a few hundred stitches removed after a particularly nasty incident with a rogue soul. I'd gotten pretty fucked up. Who am I kidding; I got bitch-slapped around like a rag-doll. The only reason I'm still alive is because Mo'Lock stepped in and saved my life.

At one point during the suture removal process, the doctor pointed out that I kept grabbing my gut. He asked me if I had stomach problems.

"I throw up a lot," I said. "Hurry up with the stitches."

The doctor bobbed his head and ran his fat tongue along the inside of his mouth. "Mr. McDonald," he said, "let's check it. Better safe than sorry, riiiiight?"

I hated him for no other reason than the way he rolled out the word "right". What a freak, and I couldn't for the life of me determine what the hell accent he had. It was either Armenian or Turkish. I couldn't decide.

I allowed him to run a few tests and poke around my gut. Every time he checked some part of me he'd shake his head. Finally after an hour he'd finished and said my stomach lining looked like Swiss cheese. I had a bleeding ulcer, acid reflux disease, and possibly a problem with my "digestive tract" or something equally disgusting. It was a polite way of saying my ass was falling apart.

"You have to take care of yourself, Mr. McDonald. You are not a young man anymore."

"Hey, fuck you!" I said, and meant it.

"Fuck me? Okay, everybody fuck me, but you have to stop drinking alcohol."

I glared at him. "Say what?"

The doctor said I had to stop eating spicy foods, quit drinking and start taking down at least a quart of milk a day. Milk. Can you believe it? I hate fucking milk. It's liquid mucus as far as I'm concerned. Just to get the asshole off my back, I agreed and left the hospital. On the way back to my house, I stopped at a corner store and picked up some milk, cigarettes, and a twelve-pack of some shit beer that was on sale. There was whiskey waiting for me on my desk.

At home, I sat at my desk and sorted through my mail while I killed one six-pack. It was nothing but a bunch of collection notices from bill collectors, as usual. I took a swig of whiskey, and I swear, because that dickhead doctor had put the idea in my head, it hurt like shit, right in the bottom of my gut. Shit. I took a bigger swig and it hurt again.

Finally, I got sick of playing tough guy with my stomach, so I started alternating shots of whiskey and milk. After about fifteen shots, I was feeling pretty normal, and then the phone rang.

I stared at the phone as it rang a couple times and debated letting it ring, but in the end I buckled and lifted the receiver.

"Yeah, hello."

It was Detective Lieutenant Gretchen Brueger. She was my LAPD contact. "I got something on the slab that I want you to look at."

"What's the job pay?"

"A big fat zero," she said

"Well, since you put it that way," I started to hang up.

"There's a reward on the case."

"I'll be there in, say, twenty minutes."

I immediately grabbed for the bottle wondering what the hell they had down there for me. Cops spook easily, so I was willing to bet that it wasn't anything too strange.

I downed another beer or two, a couple shots of whiskey, chased it all with milk, and then headed down to the

precinct to see what there was to see. It was early evening
and the heat of the daytime sun had cooled along with the
dimming light.

Inside the precinct building, I gave my name to a guy in
uniform at a desk. He said Lieutenant Brueger was waiting
for me in the morgue, and then pointed in that general
direction. I knew where it was. I'd been there before. I
walked a ways down a hall and then followed signs pointing
down a short flight of stairs. At the bottom of the stairs there
were some double doors. On the other side was the morgue.

Brueger was there waiting. She was small, but tough as
nails. You might even say she was pretty, but something
about the way she carried herself made the description
sound all wrong. There was this thing about her that said I
have a gun and I'll shoot you if you fuck with me. So I guess,
what I'm trying to say is she's pretty, but in a homicidal sort
of way.

We didn't shake hands. We just gave each other the nod.
Brueger gestured with her head for me to follow as she
pushed open another door with her shoulder. The room we
entered was a huge rectangle with plain walls, each covered
with either cabinets or bunks stacked four and five high.

On the bunks were dead bodies, most in steamy bags, but
several wore only their toe-tags. I wandered around the
room, checking out the bodies with minimal interest. I could
feel Brueger's eyes following me as I strolled. I waited a
moment, stopping in front of a John Doe, and then turned
toward her.

"So, where's this mess you want me to look at?"

She bobbed her head sideways. "This way," she said. "In
the next room."

I followed her to a door marked "Private" and we entered. The room was dim, only light from one fluorescent tube flickered on the ceiling. In the center of the room there were five bodies. All of them were covered but I could see by the size of the lumps they were small, which meant young. I could also tell by two protrusions, breasts and heads, that they were all female. Male corpses have three lumps as well, but the placement is distinctly different.

The fifth pile was short one lump. It had no head.

Brueger strolled by each body and removed the tarps that covered them. I hate to admit it, but my heart jumped a little when I saw the bodies. Or maybe a better way to describe it would be: my heart sunk.

They were dead all right. Young women, but they were a bunch of parts sewn together into bodies. Each one's head, arms, hands, torsos, legs and feet were sewn on. Most of the limbs were sewn at the joint with thick black cord and pulled tight so the skin ruffled at the bond. The folds of skin and cord sent a chill straight up the back of my neck.

I had a bad feeling about this. Not just because these poor women had been hacked up and reassembled, but because I'd seen it before. It was the specialty of a twisted fuck named Dr. Polynice. But I'd put him away twice after he'd made one too many Franken-teens and sold them as personal sex slaves.

What is up with people reanimating dead bodies? I don't get it.

These bodies were different though. First of all, there was no clear sign that any attempt had been made to reanimate the bodies. At this point, they were just chopped up and reassembled. And I'm not saying that's not strange. It's

sick as fuck, but I wasn't so sure this case required my particular area of expertise.

I turned to Brueger. "The bodies are scrambled. Maybe
it's just a way to cover the evidence or make it hard to
identify the victims."

"You tell me," she said, pointing to one of the bodies.
"This one's got that one's arm. This one's got that one's
hands. The medical examiner drew up a complete map if
you want to see it."

"What about that one?" I gestured to the headless one.
"Where's her head?"

"Look at this." Brueger moved over to a table against the
far wall.

She flicked on a desk light and there on top of the table
were two boxes.

"Two," I said.

She nodded, chewing the inside of her mouth nervously.
"Honestly, McDonald, we don't know what to think."

I nodded at the heads. "I guarantee there's another
patchwork body out there somewhere," I said.

"Right. The ME arranged the limbs on the computer.
Unscrambled, they all come together as five complete bodies,
except," she held up a finger, "each one has a missing part—
some internal as well. We thought another body like these
would turn up, but instead, we got these two heads."

I rubbed my head. "I don't see why you called me on this
one. This is weird, but not my kind of weird. Not yet."

Brueger looked annoyed. "Don't start that crap."

"I'm just saying," I said, "murder's bad and all but until
one of these dead ladies gets up and does something, it's just
a sick, twisted homicide."

Brueger seemed a tad more stressed than normal. She leaned against one of the examination tables and sighed heavily. She was collecting herself.

"Look, the Feds are moving in and taking us off the case as of seven in the morning. They're taking the bodies. I won't be able to do a thing without risking my badge."

"Well, the Feds are good at this sort of thing. They have the resources," I said, pulling out a cigarette. "Can I smoke?"

"No you can't," she barked.

I lit it anyway just to see how far I could push her. I hadn't known her all that long. I met her after I was pulled out of the drunk-tank a few months after coming to Los Angeles. She seemed cool, but you can never tell with these law enforcement types. They're as strange a lot as any. You gotta keep an eye on them. They can turn on you.

Brueger slumped. For a moment she looked like she wanted to give up. "The Feds will drag it out for years. They always do. These are local girls, Valley residents. I don't want to see any more of this. I want it stopped. The Feds are good, but they have different motives."

Her eyes were wide; all the coldness was gone.

"My hands are tied, Cal. I need you. You can do things I can't. And besides, I don't think this is a straightforward serial case. I think…"

I moved closer. "You think what?"

She shrugged. "I don't know. I just got a feeling… a really bad feeling."

"Well, leave the bad feeling for me. That's my specialty."

I nodded, turned, and scanned the bodies. They were all women, white and similar to each other in their overall appearance, each with a variation of dirty-blond hair and an athletic build. They had clearly been murdered, but for what reason, I didn't know. It didn't look like a monster case, but then again human monsters are sometimes the worst. They are certainly the most unpredictable.

I looked at Brueger, who was waiting for me to say something.

"Alright, you got me. I'm in," I said. "And you better not be lying about that reward."

She looked sideways and down. Total guilt.

"There's no reward."

She shook her head. "Sorry."

"Well, you got twenty bucks I can borrow?"

I returned to the house about an hour later with the case and a promise from Brueger to leave me to my work. She said I could use their computers if I needed them. I told her I probably wouldn't need them. Computers gave me a rash. But I might need her to make some calls for me. She agreed, but only if I kept her up to date on any progress. Whatever.

I made a gallon of coffee and downed some speed to get in the studying mood. It was some low grade meth, probably made in some redneck's basement in West Virginia. I swore to myself, speed was next on the quit list. I was getting too old to be doing hard stuff. One of these days my heart was just going to explode.

Once my scalp started to itch like it was covered with ants, I began combing through the files. The bodies had all been found on or near a jogging/walking path that ran through Runyon Park. They had all been killed the same way, and this was strange.

They had been drowned.

Runyon Park was as dry as a bone.

The medical examiner guessed they had been held under in a small pool of water such as a bath tub or even a large pan. Bruises found on three of the victims were on the backs of their necks from being forced into the water. The killer was strong. Either that or the victims trusted the killer.

There were no signs of sexual assault on any of them, no signs of robbery. If anything, the bodies were treated with extreme care. They were killed for whatever dark reason the killer had in mind, but something told me it wasn't motivated by rage or hate. There was an odd sense of caring surrounding these jigsaw women.

Brueger's report was good. It was solid. Everything seemed to be there. I doubted the Feds could do any better. I kept reading.

The victims had been cut apart and sewn together with surprising expertise, and this is where the case took the leap into weirdness that I needed: on all but one of the bodies, autopsy results showed that not only had the flesh of the bodies been put back together, but the bones and nerves had been, or attempted to be, fused together.

This was pretty advanced, sophisticated stuff. The killer was not only sewing, but doing considerably difficult surgery. I've had plenty of cases where some twisted fuck tried to make his own love doll out of dead bodies. Usually the flesh was bonded, but not much else. These women had everything mended; nerves, veins, bones. The works. They were being built to work.

I didn't want to admit it, but it looked like I had a mad genius on my hands. What I call a Franken-case.

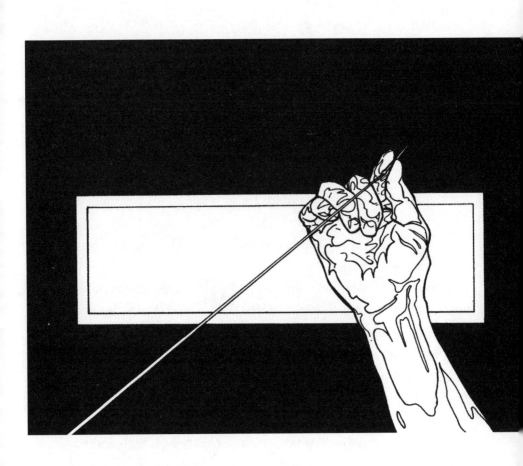

People have always tried to defeat death, but there's always a nut in the bunch who tries to create life out of death. *Frankenstein*, the book, was a story based on this concept and I'm sure Mary Shelley borrowed from something true she had heard or experienced. In the novel, Dr. Frankenstein waited for death to come and for body parts to become available, but I was afraid this killer wasn't waiting. He was killing to harvest limbs and organs. What didn't make sense was why would he dump them all.

I started to shake. Not from fear. The speed had kicked in with a vengeance. I put down the report and lit a cigarette. The room was quiet and a layer of smoke drifted around just short of eye level in the dim light. As I smoked, each drag long and deep, I sifted the facts of the case through my head.

Brueger mentioned the ME had determined that if the bodies were rearranged back to their proper order, each one would still be missing one part. Then there were the two heads in the boxes. Again, two white females. One I assumed belonged to the headless body. The other one, most likely, belonged to the jigsaw body they hadn't found, or that hadn't been dumped yet.

I was just feeling around in the dark.

I turned back to the file to investigate the victims themselves. All five, or six counting the head, were from the ages of twenty to twenty-two. They were all in college. They all disappeared on their way home from school, a week apart. The last one, the head, disappeared a week before yesterday. All the women lived within a ten mile radius of each other, but it was not yet known if any of them knew each other.

I leaned over and picked up the phone. I dialed Brueger's private line. It rang twice, and then she answered.

"Lieutenant Brueger."

"It's McDonald. I need to ask you some questions. Can we talk?"

"Not on the phone," she said quietly.

"Meet me at the Black Cat."

"That dump again?"

"They let me run a tab," I said. "See you in fifteen."

I slammed down the phone. I was jittery. I need a counter-dose. I checked the desk drawer. I was dry; no drink, no weed. I'd have to wait and grab some drinks at the Black Cat Club. I packed up my cigarettes and gun. I left the file on my desk.


Lieutenant Brueger was there waiting for me when I arrived at the club. She had a drink in front of her and shockingly, a cigarette burning between her fingers. She watched me come in and make my way toward her without ever blinking or moving. I sat down, lit a cigarette, and looked at her.

"Well?" she said.

"I might ask you the same question. Why are we meeting here?" I asked. "And why couldn't you talk on the phone?"

"The Feds showed up early. They took the bodies, the files, and I'm pretty sure they've got taps on the phones."

I raised an eyebrow. That was alarming. I haven't heard about the Feds moving that fast since JFK got his head blown out.

Brueger let out a billowing cloud of smoke followed by a hacking cough, then traded the smoke for her drink. She was trying to play it hard, but she was out of her element.

Like I said earlier, she was tough, but she was suit-tough, office-tough. Out on the streets, in a hellhole like the Black Cat, the drinks with the little pink umbrellas just didn't fly.

I thought about the file I left back at my place. "Then I have the only copy of the file. Great. You think they're on to me?"

She winced. "If they're not yet, they will be. Take care of that file. Copy it when you get a chance." She took a sip from her drink. The umbrella rolled around the edge of the glass and smacked her nose. "Now, what are these couple of things you wanted to ask?"

"Well, to start with, what tips did you guys follow up on? There wasn't much in the file about the actual investigation."

A waitress with a chain through her nose came over to us and I ordered coffee. Brueger seemed shocked. I ignored her. I was determined to stay wired. It's the only way to work these types of cases.

"What do you mean? Be specific," she asked.

"Did you do a search on other cases where decapitations were involved?"

Brueger took a final gulp of her drink. "Of course. There are no criminal cases involving decapitations on file in this area. And we went back more than twenty years."

I stewed on that a second, then said, "What about accidents?"

"I doubt there are many accidental beheadings," she laughed.

"Brueger," I said, "we only need one. Plus, if you narrow the search down to women around the age of twenty, I'm sure something will pop up."

That got her attention. "Decapitations, huh?"

"Check all kinds of accidents: cars, construction. I'm willing to gamble something comes up."

The waitress brought our drinks. My coffee smelled like old shoe. Suddenly the little umbrella drink wasn't looking so bad.

"I can't promise you anything. Records aren't filed by type of injury. What else you got?" Brueger asked, after the waitress was gone.

"This guy we're looking for definitely has some medical background. Those kids were put back together by a pro. They used methods for bonding bones that are only now being tested by surgeons. Have you run checks on medical supply houses and shit like that?"

"Yeah, but that got us nowhere. Most of those supply houses do mail order. There's no way to trace that crap. Orders vary from small town practices to major urban hospitals."

"Couldn't you narrow it down to just local small practices?" I asked. "You know, maybe they flag orders that come from homes instead of hospitals."

"Maybe," she said, shaking her head, "But records like that just aren't tracked."

"Christ, they flag teenagers for checking books of witchcraft and communism out at the library, but any jack-hole can mail-order a bone-saw and formaldehyde," I said. "Have you checked hospitals for any surgeons that have been booted for... uh, strange practices?"

"I'm with you. Yeah, we did. A big fat zero is all we got."

"What about the military, Red Cross and the like?" I asked, a little desperate.

She shook her head. "Can't get at the files. It would take months and besides, the Feds are probably checking it already."

I threw up my hands. "Well shit, I'm licked." I stood up. "Let me know what you find with those accident files. Thanks for the coffee," I said, and left.

Outside, the night air was cool. I looked forward to the walk home. Evidently, so did two guys who were following me. They were Feds. They had that stiff, cardboard, "I've got a big pole in my ass" walk. Only FBI walk like that. I think it's in their training. Evidently, the art of tailing someone isn't. They were close enough behind me that I could hear the heels of their dress shoes clicking.

I decided to take a little detour, and headed left at Coldwater instead of walking straight to my house. I came up with a little plan and I needed to find a buddy of mine, Mo'Lock.

He's a ghoul, but a hell of a nice one. When he wasn't hanging around my place he could usually be found lurking around Studio City. It had all these narrow dark alleyways. He liked that. Perfect for lurking.

Sure enough, I found him sitting outside a Starbucks talking to a few other ghouls. Mo'Lock had on his usual funeral director black suit, white shirt and black tie. The two ghouls were each wearing orange vests. They were road workers.

I made sure not to glance over my shoulder as I approached the chatting ghouls. I stopped once to light a cigarette, and behind me, I heard that their heels had stopped clicking. Jesus, these guys were dumb. Dumb or cocky. Those are the only types of Fed agents.

Mo'Lock saw me coming. He stepped up and stuck out his big boney white hand to shake mine.

"Cal. How are you? Is there trouble?" he said. "Did you know you are being followed?"

"Yeah, that's why I came here. Feel like running a little errand for me?"

"For you, Cal? Anything, any time."

"Okay, then, I need you to meet me in front of my house in around five minutes." I threw down my butt and ground it out with my heel.

The ghoul nodded. "I'll be there."

"Cool."

I started walking back towards my place. The ghoul followed me for about half a black and then disappeared into an alley.

I arrived before the ghoul did, as I'd hoped. The Feds were still on my tail, but they dropped back when I reached my place. I guess they were going to stake me out. No problem. That's what I wanted.

I went up to my house and grabbed a file out of the cabinet, then went back outside. Mo'Lock was there, waiting. He smiled when he saw me. A ghoul smiling is even creepier than one frowning. It just isn't right.

I walked up to him, holding the fake file out in the open, and handed it to him.

"I want you to take this and walk to the freeway overpass. Walk to the middle of bridge, stop, pretend to scan the papers in the file, and then throw the whole thing over the edge. That should fuck with them."

Mo'Lock looked a little confused, but he nodded. "Whatever you say, Cal" he said and walked off.

I went back inside and ran to the back window. I climbed out then crept along the wall back to the front of the house. The Feds were gone. They fell for it. They were following Mo'Lock now.

I strolled back inside. I took the file and hid it by separating the sheets of paper, rolling them, and stuffing them into the shower curtain rod in the bathroom. That would do it. Stupid Feds.

I was feeling pretty damn pleased with myself despite having done zilch on the case.

Then there was a knock at my door.

I grabbed my revolver.

"Who's there?" I said, pointing the gun at the wood just where a chest would be.

"It's me, Brueger. Open the fucking door." She was whispering.

I opened the door as she pushed past. She was out of breath, but wasted no time. She turned to me, panting and waving her finger at me.

I looked her over. "You okay?"

"I'll tell you, I thought I was nuts bringing you onto this case, but look at this." She held up a crumpled fax printout. "The computer came up with three accident related decapitations. Three!"

"I thought it would," I said. I was lying. It was a shot in the dark. Most detective work is, despite what people claim.

"Yeah, well pat your fuckin' back later. Listen, the first one is as recent as two months ago, and guess what?" She eyed me, grinning.

"Ooo, I'm breathless."

"You were involved."

"What?"

"You know all that havoc you caused when you first got here? That pile-up down near Staples Center? In the report, witnesses say they saw you running from some kind of dog..."

"It was a werewolf."

"Whatever. This wolf threw the hood of a car through the windshield of a car belonging to a Mr. Tom Davis and a Ms. Nancy Wright. Both dead. Both decapitated."

I shook my head. "They're not the ones. Next."

Brueger laughed. "You are one cocky son of a bitch."

"I know my beheadings. What about the other two?"

He fumbled with the paper. "Okay, next we got a case that happened on Mulholland."

"That's pretty close to Runyon Park," I said.

"That's right. Mulholland has one of the jogger entrances. But listen to this: a single father that goes by the name—now get this—Admiral Walter Bennington used to command one of the largest fleets in the Navy. He retired four years ago. It says in the report that three years ago he was on an outing with his daughter, Jenny, age twenty, and several other fathers and daughters. Evidently they had been white-water rafting, with the admiral's daughter in the front of the raft. Well, some local kids thought it would be humorous to tie a line of rope across the path of the rafters. It didn't work that way. The rope was too strong. Jenny Bennington was decapitated."

"And they never found the head," I said. "That sucks."

"You got it, but there's more. Admiral Bennington spent time during Vietnam working in the ship's hospital."

"Lots of amputations, I'm sure," I said. Brueger nodded. "And there's that drowning/water connection, too."

"You're just smart as the dickens, aren't you?" said Brueger. "That, and the medical background puts Bennington in the prime suspect column."

"What about number three?"

"A little more cut and dried. Divorced father, Tom Burns, is driving on the 101 with his nineteen year old daughter, Trisha. There's some kind of confusion, and the car loses control. The top of the car is ripped clean off and the kid's head goes with it. The father suffers minor injuries, but..."

I cut in, "They never found the head."

"Right."

"A highway accident and they can't find a girl's head?"

"Evidently."

"This stinks like all hell. What's this Burns's record like? What'd he do for a living?"

"You ready for this? He's a bio-engineer. Still is. He's one of those fucks trying to genetically alter vegetables and fish. He was supposed to retire last year, but after his kid got killed, he decided to stay on."

Both men sounded suspicious as fuck, but what were the odds? The Valley is a big place and Los Angeles is fucking huge. Was it possible that two men who lost their daughters could meet?

It was going to be a matter of checking each of them out and seeing how they ticked. The Feds were bound to run a check on accidental decapitations sooner or later, so I wanted to beat them to it.

I looked at Brueger.

"If we're going to do anything, we have to move tonight," I said. "I say we split up. Bennington has all this medical experience and this Burns guy... It really bugs me they didn't find the daughter's head. I mean, Christ, how do you lose a head on a highway?"

"Okay, let's say we flip a coin. See who gets who." She already had a coin in her hand. "Heads the Admiral, tails the bio-engineer. You call it." She threw the coin into the air.

"Tails."

The coin landed. She flipped it onto her forearm. "Heads. You lose. You get Burns."

Perfect. He would have access to all kinds of lab and medical equipment and I just couldn't shake the idea of them not finding his kid's head. It was just a little weird. I stood up and put on my gun. I noticed Brueger was picking up the phone.

"What are you doing?"

"Calling in to the station. I want to see if the sixth body has turned up yet. Don't worry; I worked out a code with the desk sergeant. The Feds won't know what the hell we're talking about."

"Don't bother. There isn't going to be a sixth body." I said.

Brueger stared at me for a second, hesitated, and then hung up the phone.

She walked over toward me, ripping the fax sheet in half. "Here's Burns's address. No matter what happens, we meet back here." she glanced at her watch. "In two hours. That'll be about three-thirty."

"Right," I said as we left the building.

Brueger went to her car, while I walked to the curb and hopped into mine. Burns lived in North Hollywood. It was

just down the street, and smack in the middle between the
accident and Runyon Canyon.

I wasn't surprised to see the house when I pulled up. It
was a big detached deal, two stories with yard and pool. I
guess bio-engineers make a pretty penny. Who knew there
was money in making giant mutant food?

I got out of the car and stood, staring at the house. The
entire second floor was dark, but there were several lights lit
on the first floor. There were two cars in the driveway. Both
had California tags. I made my way up the drive.

As I passed the first car, I stopped and stared down at a
sticker on the back window. I was glad I lost the coin toss.

I made my way around to the back of the house with my
gun out. I was willing to bet the place had a basement and
that was where the action would be. I found a back door,
scanned the glass for alarm tape, and then picked the lock
with a phone card. It opened easily.

I stood silently in the open doorway, waiting to hear if
there was a dog in the house. Nothing lunged and ripped my
throat out so I moved in, sliding the door closed behind me.
I was in the kitchen and not less than six feet from me was
the basement door with light coming from under it.

I edged quietly over to it and pressed my ear to the wood.
There were voices, two of them, and they were having one
hell of an argument.

"...you have to be patient. Memory is tricky. It's going to
take a while!"

"I'm not paying you to be patient. I want results and I
want them now!"

It was worse and weirder than I thought. I had to make a move. I only hoped they weren't armed. I began to reach for the doorknob when I heard the sound of feet on the stairs. Someone was coming.

I moved swiftly into the house, glanced around and saw stairs. I tip-toed up as fast as I could without making a sound and stood, listening.

Someone opened the basement door. I couldn't tell where they were or what they were doing. Then I saw someone appear at the bottom of the stairs.

And he saw me.

Shit, shit, shit.

It was a balding man. He looked stunned, and when he saw my gun he shot from stunned to shaking.

I pointed it at him. "Don't move! Police!" I yelled.

But he didn't listen. They never do. He bolted off back toward the basement. I had a clear shot at him for a good couple seconds, but curiosity wouldn't let me pull the trigger.

"Bennington!" he yelled.

I fucked up. I looked around. There was a dim light coming from beneath a door down the hall. I ran toward it and went in, slamming the door shut behind me. I heard feet, four of them, running up the basement stairs. They were rushing, confident, which meant they were armed. This was not what I planned. After a lifetime of fighting monsters I was going to get shot by my two dads. Fuck!

I looked around the room I was in. It was a girl's room. I say this not because it was pink or anything like that. It was clean. Boys rooms are never clean, and this room was pristine. It looked like it hadn't been touched in years.

Then I saw the half empty glass of milk. I wasn't alone in the room.

I lowered my gun. The closet was partially open. Hearing the voices coming closer, I moved and pushed the closet open.

Crumpled naked on the floor and shivering was the sixth body.

She was alive, all balled up in a fetal position.

I knelt down. The kid looked up at me. She didn't seem afraid. Her face was stark white with blue lips and yellowed eyes.

They hadn't preserved the head very well.

"Are you Jenny?" I whispered.

The patchwork girl shook her head. "Jenny's dead. I'm Trisha. Are you here to help me?"

I nodded, glancing quickly over her body; a web of thick cord holding patches of flesh in place. "I'm going to try," I said.

Outside the door, I could hear that they were right there, whispering a plan to each other.

I looked at the kid. "Don't worry about what I'm about to say, okay? Understand?"

Jigsaw Trisha nodded.

I turned toward the door. "All right, Bennington, Burns! I've got a gun and I've got the girl!"

There was no reply. I put my hand out to Trisha. She took it and I helped her to her feet. Each part had a slightly different tint. I grabbed a robe out of the closet and wrapped her in it. She nodded and looked at me doe-eyed, like a suffering animal waiting to die.

"Come on, we're going to get out of here," I whispered. And I meant it.

The door flew open. The crazy fucks bum-rushed me, and it worked! They caught me completely off guard. I was helping the kid, the room was small and they crashed into me, both of them, and dragged me to the floor. My gun dropped out of my hand. The bald guy, Burns, pummeled my face while the other man, Bennington I assumed, kicked me in the stomach.

I was down for the count. I had no air and the speed only made it worse.

They had me pinned and each of them had guns. They were old men, but the guy I guessed was Bennington was big and burly. He leaned into my face.

"Who are you? Who sent you?" he spat.

I didn't say a word. I just looked at them. God, I fucking wanted to kill them.

He repeated his question. I stayed quiet.

Bennington pounded his fist into the side of my face. It felt like a hammer.

I dug a hunk of torn cheek out of my bleeding mouth and spit the glob right into Bennington's face. It stuck on his forehead like a spitball until he wiped it away.

Behind them, Trisha was bending down.

The other guy, Burns, slugged me across the face with the butt of his gun and was about to do it again when his head sort of exploded. One second he had a face, the next it was a red pile of goop.

I didn't wait to see what happened.

The woman had my gun and was staring down at the gory mess that was on top of me. I pushed it aside. I was covered with blood and brains. I was watching the Admiral. He had the gun on Trisha.

"I'm gonna kill the girl! I'm gonna kill the little monster, do you hear me!"

I got to my feet and raised my hands. I was the only one alive in the room who didn't have a gun.

"Trisha," I said, "just stay calm and I'll get us out of here, OK?"

The patchwork woman looked at me and tilted her head. "I'm Jenny. Trisha died in an accident."

Uh oh.

Bennington, the fucking admiral started to cry. "I can't kill Jenny! I can't!"

I leaned in. "How about everybody lower their weapons."

I held out my hands and waited for one of them to hand me their gun.

Bennington shuddered and bawled like a baby. Snot streamed over his mouth. He kept the gun on the young dead woman. "I don't want to kill you."

And then Trisha, Jenny, and the others spoke.

"We don't care what you do. We want to die. You already killed us once," she said, her voice low and controlled.

Bennington's eyes were as wide as mine and he responded as I would have. "We?" he said. His gun-hand was shaking violently and sweat gathered on his forehead.

The girl took a step toward him. "You're not my father. You're my killer," she said.

"I didn't kill you, baby," he whined. "It was an accident."

She pointed to her hip where the flesh appeared tanner than the rest. "You killed Stephanie and Sally and Beth... killed all of us."

They didn't even know I was there. It was the jigsaw girl's moment and I let her have it, or more to the point I let them have their moment with their killer. I believed Bennington hadn't killed his daughter, but he lost her and the grief drove him to murder other girls for parts.

Maybe he met Burns by accident, maybe they sought each other out. It didn't matter. Two fathers had lost their daughters. Both heads had never been found. I looked at the girl and saw the stitching around the back of her head. I guessed that the head was one daughter's and the brain the other's.

The patchwork woman raised the gun and clenched her teeth. "We're going to kill you now."

Bennington pissed himself and sobbed. He let the gun slip from his hands. It was finally too much. He surrendered.

But this seemed to upset the girl all the more. As I reached for Bennington's dropped weapon I felt a stinging pain shoot through the back of my head. I knew what it was. I'd been there a thousand times before. The jigsaw girl had knocked me out.


I woke later in a pool of meat and blood.

My heart jumped. I sat up and pulled myself off the floor and out of the gore. My head pounded, and my tongue throbbed metallic. When my eyes finally focused I saw the blood.

Spattered on the ground below was Bennington, his head smashed open, his body bent like a rag doll. Scratch marks and bullet holes covered what wasn't torn.

But no jigsaw girl. Trisha, Jenny, Sally; whoever she was, she was gone.

Behind me, I heard someone suck air.

"Hi, Brueger. What took you so long?"

Brueger came over and helped me to my feet. It was the first time she had touched me, and it felt pretty good. It felt real and alive.

"You did it."

I glared at her. "I didn't do anything but get my ass kicked."

"I looked in the basement. There's proof: photos, plans, everything."

I turned and faced her. There were about ten thousand wise cracks I could have thrown out, but I felt sick. I just nodded and started walking out of the house.

Brueger seemed confused at my lack of excitement. Then she looked around the room.

"Any luck finding the sixth body? It wasn't in the basement."

I saw the bloody footprints in the hallway, seeping into the plush white carpet, and leading to the stairs.

"Brueger, trust me on this one. You don't want to know."

## The End

Eater

# I think it was Tuesday.

It didn't really matter. I don't exactly keep a nine-to-five schedule. I was lying face down on the floor, fully dressed, about three feet from my door when the phone woke me up. Each ring ripped through my spongy skull and drilled straight through to my brain like an electric charge.

Next to me was a puddle of vomit I didn't even remember throwing up. At the moment I was just glad I wasn't lying in it. I've been there before and it's a nasty way to wake up.

I didn't remember how I got home. I had been drinking at a bar; I'm not sure which bar it was. It was probably the Black Cat Club. It had become my favorite drinking hole for a couple reasons. One, it had the same name as the club I hung out at in DC. Two, they let my tab run for six months without once asking me to pay. God bless the Black Cat Club.

After I crawled to my feet, nimbly avoiding the circle of puke, I looked out the window. The Catalina was safe and parked at the curb. It was parked straight and there weren't any trees, signs, or bodies smashed in the grill, so wherever I went, I must have walked home afterwards. There are about thirty dive bars in Studio City. For all I know, I hit every one. It wouldn't be the first time. I tend to stick to the BC, but I like to go to other bars to scan for freaks.

I touched my face and it stung like a motherfucker. It felt swollen and suddenly it all started coming back to me in slow, stomach-turning flashbacks. I remember popping some pills. Then I had a few shots. From there—and I was still home at this point—things got a little fuzzy.

I know I got into a fist fight with just about everyone in one place. They threw me out. I went to another bar, and started another fight with some Zeppo Marx-haired LA slickster in a red satin pirate shirt who bumped into me. He gave me some attitude so I dragged him into the bathroom and slammed his head into the urinal until I was tackled from behind and thrown out.

The phone rang and rang, louder than I ever recall hearing it. It sounded like a cathedral bell was right next to my head with a little hunchback swinging and yelling. My head was about to split open, and it wouldn't stop. I took out my revolver, gave the phone one warning, and then shot it.

The bang hurt even worse. I'm a fucking retard.

Besides, the phone wasn't dead, even with a slug through its mechanical body. It still rang. I had to stop it. I was Baretta. The living room was the hood of a car. I lunged across the room, almost slipping in the puke, and reached for the cradle before it could squeeze off another brain-crippling ring.

"What in God's name do you want?" I said.

There was a long silence. Whatever dickhead was on the other end knew he was playing with his life.

"Cal, it's me, Mo'Lock."

It was the ghoul. He had a knack for calling at exactly the wrong time. But he had done me right too many times for me to blow him off. He'd pretty much set himself as my partner when he followed me from the East Coast out to Los Angeles. That was one dedicated dead guy. You hadda love him.

Well, at least tolerate his weird ass.

"Where are you?" I said, looking around the house for clues, still trying to figure out how I got home. All I had was; drinking, drugs, fight... blank.

The ghoul said, "I'm right around the corner." He sounded excited, which, coming from a creepy-ass ghoul, was kind of scary.

I could feel a volcano of bile and beer rumbling in my stomach.

"Um, uh, give me a few minutes. I gotta throw up," I said, and then followed with, "Did you see me last night?"

"No. I was at the reservoir."

I started to ask why, but thought better of it and slammed the phone back into the cradle.

I bolted for the bathroom like an all-star sprinter. I almost crossed the finish line, too, but just as I ran through the bathroom doorway, I projectile vomited, sending a sickening (and strangely perfect) arcing fountain through the air. I must've looked like one of those water spouts people put in their yards to tell the world they're rich and have bad taste.

Funny thing was, most of the puke actually landed in the toilet. Years of throwing up perfects one's aim, I guess.

Half-dead, I climbed into the shower and let hot water pummel my aching head until I got my eyes most of the way open. I felt like hell, but I'd felt a lot worse. At least I wasn't suffering from any major injuries for once. Things had been pretty quiet lately. There had been a vampire skulking around Silverlake a couple weeks back, but I tracked him down and killed him in the same night. Jack-hole.

Most of my free time I spent with Sabrina Lynch. I guess you could say the two of us were going out. She runs a little rag about unexplained phenomena called *Speculator Magazine*. She used to trash me all the time, calling me some kind of fraud, but now that we're sleeping together she's backed off.

She was off somewhere for the past week, thank God. I recall her mentioning some crop circles or a Chupacabra sighting in Mexico she wanted to cover for the magazine. She did everything for the magazine pretty much herself. It was damned impressive.

Just as I finished dressing, there was a knock. I walked over and pulled open the door. It was Mo'Lock. In his arms he had something bundled up in a blanket.

The bundle was moving.

I was in no mood for surprises or moving bundles.

"Come on in," I said in my best fake-happy voice. "What's that you got there?"

"That's why I came. I don't know what it is." The ghoul lumbered past me into the office.

I didn't pay much attention. I didn't even look at the bundle. I was still asleep. "I'm making coffee. You want some?"

"No," he said, but he wasn't looking at me. He was staring down at the pool of vomit on the floor. "What's this?"

"Chicken and dumplings. Help yourself." I got my coffee; actually I just grabbed the pot, and sat at my desk. "So, let's see what you got."

Mo'Lock stepped up to the desk with his bundle and laid it on the desktop. It was pretty big for a small bundle, about the size of two stacked soccer balls, inside a canvas sack. The sack was tied off with some thick cord.

Then the ghoul untied it and revealed the contents.

I shot up from my desk.

"AAAAAGGHH, what is that thing? Get it the fuck off my desk!"

Mo'Lock held up his hand. "Relax. It's only a baby."

"A baby what?!"

The ghoul explained in calm detail how he had come to possess the creature. The story was strange, but it made sense and I believed him. I'd heard stranger.

The way the ghoul told it, he was crawling around in the sewers with some of his ghoul buddies doing God knows what and they came across this big brown humanoid hippo-looking creature that had been injured. Turned out the creature's wounds were fatal, and after giving birth to the thing on my desk, the big creature died. Mo'Lock took the baby.

"We couldn't just leave it there," the ghoul said, wrapping up his story.

I looked at the thing on my desk. "Sure you could've. You just didn't."

I studied the small creature on my desk while I drank from the pot of coffee. It was around three and a half feet long, dark brown in spots, but mostly a light gray-green. It was bulky looking and its hide looked pretty tough, like rhino skin or maybe crocodile. Its mouth was wide and when it opened, I could see double rows of tiny but sharp as shit teeth. Its nose was nothing more than two punctures above wide lips and the eyes were the same except bigger and completely red with small black pin-sized pupils.

Mo'Lock told me how big the dead mother had been and I could only imagine how large this little shit was going to be.

"It's grown since this morning," Mo'Lock said.

Great.

I stared at the thing a little more. It kept moving its mouth over and over. Open close, open close. I looked at Mo'Lock. "I think it's hungry."

"What do you think it eats?" he asked.

"I don't even know what it is. How the fuck am I supposed to know what it eats?"

I was a bit frazzled. It had been peaceful lately and I wasn't really in the mood for anything like this. I'm not the goddamn Humane Society, for Christ's sake. What was I supposed to do? Then again, I thought, it was probably better that I deal with the creature before it got bigger.

Knowing my luck, it would probably come after me when it was as big as a house.

"I think I have a plan," I said.

Mo'Lock lit up. "Yeah?"

"Let's kill it."

"Cal!" exclaimed the ghoul. He looked really upset at the suggestion.

"Okay, okay, it was just an idea." I looked down at the thing. It was kind of cute in an ugly sort of way. "What do you think we should feed it?"

I put my finger a little too close to its mouth.

It chomped down. I screamed, stiffened, and slapped its head until it let go. By the time I got my finger free, the little fuck had gotten away with at least a half-inch of my left hand index finger. Blood got all over the place until Mo'Lock handed me a cloth and I wrapped it up. But it still hurt.

Mo'Lock smiled sheepishly. "Well, at least we know what it eats."

I glared at him and told him there was some ground beef in the fridge that was only a little moldy. He went and got it while I studied the creature and tried to figure out what the hell we were going to do with it. My first plan was still sounding pretty good.

The ghoul came back from the kitchen area with the beef and the creature proceeded to eat it. It took the mound out of his hand and then, I swear, it sat up and devoured the entire hunk in a single swallow.

Mo'Lock and I stood there staring and, as if that wasn't enough, it grew. Right there in front of our eyes, it grew. It just sort of expanded. It licked its lips, rubbed its face, and then looked up at me, then Mo'Lock, as though asking for more.

I glanced over at the ghoul, who was looking less confident than usual. Good. I was pissed. Fucking stupid, do-gooding ghoul.

"This is really fucked up, Mo'," I said. "Why don't we call someone who can tell us what we're dealing with here?"

His sheep-face expression changed into a more cocky version. "Like who, Cal? Rod Serling is dead."

I actually started laughing. Where the hell did a ghoul hear about *The Twilight Zone*? They probably showed episodes at undead training seminars. Who the fuck knows?

I started pacing around the office, occasionally looking at the thing on my desk. It had grown when we fed it. That really freaked me out. Time was a factor. The mother was the size of a hippo and she was female. Chances were males grew even bigger, and the little bastard had a set of balls and hole that probably housed a little gray dick.

My brain was just too cluttered. I was hung over as all hell and trying to think of what to do with the little creep was just making it worse. I needed a drink, but the apartment was dry.

I told Mo'Lock to stay with the thing while I ran to the liquor store. Hair of the dog that bit me. That would do the trick.

I ran a bit late getting back to Mo'Lock and the creature. I wound up drinking half the bottle I'd purchased while I drove home, so I turned back around and bought another one. The clerk at the store said he'd give me a discount on cases. I sneered at him. I should've clocked him. Fucking dick.

It really pissed me off when some asshole butt-fuck thought it was his right to get into my shit. I mean, I'd never consider walking up to someone on the street and telling them what I thought. Oh well, screw it. Most people don't know half the shit that's going on around them anyway. If they did, they'd have a heart attack.

I made my way back to my place about forty-five minutes after I'd left. I ambled my way up the stairs, sensing something almost instantly. There was something very wrong ahead of me. I got to my porch when the scent rolled beneath my nostrils. Blood and lots of it... coming from inside.

I shifted my parcel into my left arm and took out my revolver. I slid along the outside of the house, moving quietly so that I could hear any noise that might be coming from inside. The sounds I heard were strange and unnatural. There was a sort of sloshing, followed by a wet slap, then more sloshing.

I got right outside my door and made my move. I hate putting things like this off. I kicked in the door. It flew open and the smell of blood grew thicker. My office was covered with it, and I mean fuckin' everywhere. The walls and floor were smeared sticky red.

And there in the middle of the room was Mo'Lock, with a mop.

He looked up at me. There was a hint of fear in his hollow eyes, and beneath them, a slack-jawed guilty mouth.

"I can explain," he said.

I almost dropped my bag, but instead put it on the floor, slowly, as I kicked the door shut. I kept my gun in hand. I could feel my body shaking, but I couldn't tell whether I was scared or mad. I made a sort of side-swipe gesture with my head telling the ghoul to get on with the explaining.

He stood there holding the mop, covered in blood the way a spastic kid gets covered with mud. "Well, you had a client stop by. A new one, I think, and well, she came to the door..."

That was all I needed to hear. I was looking around the room. "Where's that little fuck?"

"It's in the bathroom," said Mo'Lock. "It was a woman and I managed to lock the thing in the bathroom before she saw it... and well... while I was explaining that you were running an errand... the thing got out of the bathroom."

I ran my tongue against the inside of my mouth. "It locks from the inside."

"The creature ran right at her. I tried to get it off, but before I knew what was happening it had ripped her head off and blood was spraying everywhere. It was horrible, Cal. Her body was flopping around while the thing practically swallowed her head whole."

I just stood there staring, stunned, at the ghoul.

"I didn't know what to do, Cal. Honest. So when the thing started eating the rest of the body, I figured, you know—what is that phrase you use? What the hell, at least it gets rid of the body, right? Right, Cal? Why are you looking at me like that?"

I tried very hard to maintain control, but I was going to explode. I held one finger up in the air. "Now, let me get this straight. I may have gotten the first paying client I've had in months and that little mystery pig ate her?"

Mo'Lock nodded. "Yeah, that's pretty much the story."

That did it. I pulled the hammer back on my gun and headed toward the bathroom. "Okay, okay, here we go. The mystery is solved! You want to know what that thing is... it's soon to be deceased! How's that?!"

Mo'Lock jumped in front of me. "No, Cal! Don't!" He had his arms spread out, blocking my path. "I can see why you're upset, but killing that baby won't solve anything."

"It'll solve EVERYTHING, you idiot!"

The ghoul wouldn't let me past and he knew I wasn't going to fight him. "Come on, calm down. Have a drink. Take a pill. Smoke something." He smiled a strained, dead man's smile.

He knew me too well.

I nodded and put my gun away. "Any idea who this woman was?"

Mo'Lock pointed to my desk. "I've been trying to clean the blood. Her purse is over there."

I grabbed one of the bottles from the bag on the floor, locked the front door and went to my desk. The purse was red Prada, ultra-shiny leather and had a diamond studded clasp. Great. She was rich, too. Or rather, used to be rich.

She had probably come to me so she could pay me out the nose to follow her husband. He was most likely cheating on her and she wanted the upper hand in the divorce. All I would have had to do was get some pictures of an old fat-ass porking some eighteen-year-old and I'd have been set for a year. Just my luck she'd gotten herself eaten.

I opened the bottle first and chugged it down a good inch. It burned the shit out of my ulcer, but felt perfect flowing into my brain. I could feel my heart rate steady. I grabbed the purse, unclasped it, and then dumped the contents onto my desk blotter. Contents as follows: a handkerchief with the initials AMN embroidered in the corner, a Prada wallet of matching red leather, a keychain with one sort of bulky key on it, some scattered change, and some lint.

I picked up the wallet. It folded open long-ways. First, I found her ID and saw her picture. She was gorgeous. Dark hair, full lipped and eyes that said: "I'm really rich and beautiful so forget I am a loser."

Her name was Annette Miles Newman, which meant nothing to me. The ID was new, only about two weeks old. There were a ton of credit cards and a little cash. I took it. I took everything out and as I pulled out the last plastic card, a bus ticket stub fell onto the blotter. It said Arizona.

Now, that was strange. What would a woman with as much dough as she obviously had be doing with a bus ticket? And from Arizona, no less. Who the fuck would live in Arizona?

I looked at everything in front of me. It all, except for the stub, looked pretty straight. Then I noticed the key. I picked it up. It was plastic, not flexible toy plastic, but hard and smooth. That was strange, but it was probably some rich people thing. I wouldn't know. I've never been rich. I put the plastic key in my pocket just in case. Then I gathered all the stuff and threw it into a plastic bag.

Mo'Lock was mopping away, but didn't really seem to be making much progress. "Hey, why don't you just let the little fuck lick it up?"

I was joking, but the ghoul didn't get the joke. He nodded, impressed with the idea and went to the bathroom and opened the door. The thing came waddling out. It was bigger, almost a foot bigger, and its body had a lot more bulk. It looked at me. I gave it the finger.

Mo'Lock gave its head a little push toward the floor. It fought at first, but then after sniffing the pools, began lapping them up. It was disgusting watching the thing go at it, but it was doing the trick.

Mo'Lock smiled at me. "Good idea, Cal."

I wanted to throw up again. Let the little fuck lick that up.

It took a few hours but eventually, with the help of the mystery beast, the place got cleaned up (and it even ate my vomit from the night before). I kept a close eye on the thing, knowing that sooner or later it was going to try to escape or take a swipe at me. Every once in a while it would sniff at me, then look away when I flipped it off. It was nearly twice the size it had been this morning.

Mo'Lock kept pacing around the room while I drank and smoked myself into a nifty stupor. I had no idea what to do about the creature but my concern was nowhere near as great as the ghoul's.

"We've got to think of something," he said. "We've gotten nowhere."

I was drunk. "I stand by Plan A. Let's put the little bastard on a spit and roast him."

The ghoul got pissy and ignored me for the next hour. I didn't really care. Fuck him. He's the one who got us into the mess in the first place.

Mo'Lock was sitting and pouting at the window when the limousine pulled up to the curb outside the building. I had started going to work on the second bottle and was riding a pretty hard buzz.

He turned to me. "Cal, come here and look at this."

I got up, fell back into the chair, tried again. Once I got my footing, I went to the window. The back door of a huge, shiny black limo was being held open by an equally huge bald guy at the curb in front of the house.

I sobered a bit and turned to the ghoul. "Get into my room with that thing and keep it quiet while I deal with this," I said.

I immediately began scanning the room for blood or anything else that might give us away. Outside, I heard footsteps clicking up the walkway. I fast tip-toed over to the door and gently unlocked it. Behind me, Mo'Lock, with the creature in hand, shut the bedroom door. I tip-toed back to my desk and kicked over my trash can by accident. It made a tremendous noise, but I was sitting by the time the knock came at the door.

"Come in!" I yelled.

And in they came; three of them. I first noticed the two gigantic, oddly identical looking thugs. They were the twin towers of goons. In front of them was a little crotchety old man—their boss, I assumed—who looked like he'd soaked in salt water for a month, then been rolled in a ball and pounded with a mallet until every inch of his flesh wrinkled.

The thugs were scanning the room with a secret-police arrogance that set my temper off quickly. It didn't help matters that I was inebriated. Fortunately, the old man spoke before I let my anger show or pulled out my gun and started shooting.

The old man's voice was just plain creepy; somewhere between Boris Karloff and Mr. Rogers. "Are you Mr. McDonald?"

"That's what it says on the audit."

"I am looking for my wife. She said she was coming to see you today."

I shook my head and shrugged. "Well, I wouldn't know anything about that. I was out all day," I lied. "Maybe there's something else I could help you with?"

The old man hobbled forward, narrowing his eyes. "You are a very bad liar, Mr. McDonald. A child could see through your charade."

I stood up. "Hey! Fuck you! Who the hell do you—"

The goons began to step toward me. I whipped out my gun and raised it. That didn't stop the giants so I pulled back the hammer.

"Okay, you old fuck," I said, "tell your bookends to back off!"

The old guy raised his hand. The goons stopped in their tracks like giant wind-up toys. "There's no need for violence," he said. "Yet."

I waved the gun in their faces. "Fun's over. I hate you all. I see no future in this relationship." I pointed the gun right at the old man. I had to close one eye to focus. "Now get the fuck out of my office!"

There was a moment of frozen, tense silence. I was breathing so hard I could smell my own liquor breath. I thought they might actually attack me or something. But instead the old wrinkly guy just sort of shrugged, though it looked more like a hiccup, and waved his hand at the goons. Without a word the trio walked out of the house and slammed the door behind them.

I waited a couple beats, then... "They're gone. You can come out now."

Mo'Lock lumbered out with the creature at his side. His hand was on its shoulder. "That was weird," the ghoul said.

I nodded and looked at him. "Yeah, a little too weird."

I didn't want to alarm the ghoul, but that little old man and his twin freaks set off every inner alarm I relied on. There was something unnatural about all three of them, but it wasn't anything I'd ever dealt with before.

It was something new.

I pointed at the ghoul. "You want to stay or run recon?"

Mo'Lock looked at the creature standing against his leg. "I better stay here."

"Right," I said and went to the front door.

I eased the door open. The street was clear... until I stepped onto the porch. The limo had only moved a few yards down the street. I ducked quickly and made like a spy, edging along the fence, crawling over the neighbor's fence, and then skulking along that yard until I was within earshot of the limo.

Then all three got out of the car. They scanned the area. They didn't see me.

The two goons stood side by side in the shadows in front of the old man.

One of the thugs spoke first. "The animal was there."

"Yes, I know," the old man said. "And she was there as well, or had been at one time. That disgusting detective was lying about more than just the animal."

Disgusting? Screw that fuck. I hoped his diapers broke.

The other goon spoke. He had the same exact voice as goon number one. "Why didn't we just take it, then?" he asked.

"Because, idiot, if the detective knows anything about Annette's whereabouts, we don't want him dead yet. Annette has the key."

The goons nodded their bald heads in unison.

The old man grumbled for a second or two, then made a decisive grunt. "I want you to spy on the detective."

"Now?" both asked.

"Yes, now. Shift into Spy Mode."

Spy Mode? What the fuck? I couldn't resist. I slowly peered up through the chain-link fence. There were shrubs obscuring my view, but I could see the goons facing their boss.

Both goons went rigid and closed their eyes. Each exhaled long and controlled breaths. On about the third breath, their bodies just froze. It was so sudden and so stiff I thought I was seeing things. They were absolutely still, like a machine turned off.

If only it had stopped there.

Then the tops of their heads began to part and the fronts of their eyelids went soft as the heads lost their contents. The heads parted smoothly in two parts; first the skin split and opened, exposing the skulls beneath, and then they, in turn, did the same.

Their brains were visible.

I think I almost pissed myself. I didn't need to see anymore. I turned away and crawled back the same way I

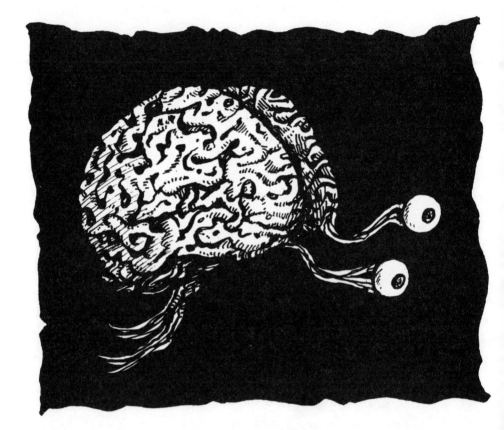

came until I reached my house. Inside Mo'Lock sat on the couch with the ugly little creature next to him.

"We've got big trouble," I said.

Mo'Lock tilted his head, "How do you mean?"

"I have no idea."

When I get scared or freaked out, it turns to anger pretty fucking fast. I was really pissed. I mean, first this orphan flesh-eater devours a potential client, now threats from a thousand-year-old man and his thugs.

I had sobered up, so I tried to finish off the bottle. It wasn't working. My stomach was raging and every shot I took felt like a fire in my gut. I didn't really have a plan for the evening, but all of this was not it.

Mo'Lock was pacing around the room and the little thing watched his every move. Finally, after a couple hundred laps around the office, he stopped and turned to me. The ghoul opened his mouth to talk, but instead, he just sort of froze. His eyes weren't on me, but the window behind me.

I turned around.

"Oh, give me a fucking break," I said.

There, floating outside, were two sets of prying eyes dangling from two flying brains. I assumed the brains had come from the skulls of the old man's goons.

That was it. I'd seen everything.

I jumped to my feet and my gun was in hand in an instant. I fired right through the window. Glass shattered, mixing with smoke from the blasts. The little creature behind me started squealing like a pig.

"Shut that little bastard up!" I yelled.

I couldn't tell if I'd hit anything at all, and it didn't matter. Before I knew it, the client-eating creature ran past me and jumped out the window. Mo'Lock yelled after it, but it was gone, as were the flying brains.

The office was quiet.

I looked at Mo'Lock. His mouth was still open.

"Can we stop now?" I asked. "Any more of this shit and my head's going to explode."

"We can't leave it out there. It will kill everything it comes across."

The big dead freak was right. I jammed my gun back under my shoulder and with me leading, we left the house. We didn't get very far. Outside we found out I was a better shot than I thought. One of the brains was on the sidewalk. I'd blown a decent chunk out of it. It wasn't moving.

"Check it out. I killed the brain."

Mo'Lock looked at the dead brain. "I have never seen anything like this before, have you?"

"Nope."

I was about to bend over for a closer look when all of a sudden there was the sound of screeching wheels and people screaming nearby.

I shot a look at the ghoul. "The thing?!"

He nodded and we both bolted toward the commotion. We were running up my street, headed toward Laurel Canyon Boulevard. I could see up ahead that there had been an accident. I prayed the thing had been mowed down.

As we ran, I turned and glanced over my shoulder. The other brain was following us. I yelled for Mo'Lock to keep going. I swung around, pulled my gun in a single motion, and fired at the spy brain. It swooped left, then right, dodging the shots perfectly. That brain really knew how to fly. I took a couple more shots at it, but didn't aim too carefully. The brain avoided those as well. I was wasting my time.

I reached the street just as the ghoul was crossing it. He stopped and turned to me, pointing ahead.

There was the little thing, only about a block ahead of us. We ran on and I caught up with the ghoul.

I looked over at him as we ran. "You run ahead. It trusts you. See if you can get it in the park."

I glanced over my shoulder. The brain was hot on my tail, and not only that, but I saw the old man's black limo moving past the intersection toward us. I just kept running but I cut to a slower pace.

Within seconds, I could feel the brain on my neck. That's what I wanted and I kept moving. The Hugh Beaumont Memorial Park was just ahead. Mo'Lock was already there. I kept up the deliberately slow pace until I was right at the edge of the park grounds. Then I made my move. I swung around, snatched the brain in mid-air and pulled it down. It fought me but I was stronger. I tucked the brain under my arm like a football, turned back and sprinted into the park for what I hoped would be the winning score.

Mo'Lock was there waiting with the creature next to him. I ran up to them.

We heard a car door slam. I went up to the ghoul, then turned and waited. I had my gun on the brain.

It was a standoff.

Of course old man took his sweet-ass time. I yawned at least once waiting for him to hobble within sight. The old man was smiling. He saw I had the gun on the brain, but didn't seem too concerned.

"Don't move!" I yelled. "Or the brain gets it."

The old man stepped forward. "Oh come now, Mr. McDonald. There's no reason for theatrics. Just give me the animal and I'll be off."

Huh? The animal? Did he mean our miniature flesh-eater? I looked at Mo'Lock, who was glancing sideways at me. He looked just as confused. We had no idea what was going on.

The old guy took another step. "Please, there's very little time," he said. "And, I wonder if you might tell me what happened to Annette?"

"Pig-Baby ate her," I said.

"Oh dear," the old man said rubbing his chin. "That does present a problem."

"Yeah, how's that?"

The old fart looked at me with a static stare. "I suppose it's time we all come clean. I assume you have the key, then? Am I right?"

Fuck it, I thought. This guy knew what was happening. I didn't. Part of wading through the murk of the macabre is knowing when to throw in the towel. I pulled the key out of my pocket, letting the brain go. It flew back to the old man. I threw him the key.

"This was part of the deal I had with Annette," he said. "She knew I couldn't leave without the key."

As he spoke he worked the key under his collar until we heard a loud cracking sound. Then he turned it and the skin of his head split open. He grabbed it with both hands and tore it back and off. It all became a little clearer when I saw his real face.

He was a greenish-gray, with no nose or ears. He had huge eyes that blinked slowly and smoothly. Just like those stupid

UFO drawings you see in the tabloids. The head was a lot smaller then you'd think, but I guess compared to the skinny body it was a pretty large melon.

All I could think about was Sabrina off in Mexico taking pictures of crop circles, and I had the real deal right in front of me. She was gonna shit.

The old man alien-thing reached into his pocket without moving his big blinking eyes from us. He pulled out a device that was about the size and shape of a television remote, and pointed it at us.

I jumped a bit. Mo'Lock, beside me, stepped forward just a touch. It was his way of saying he had my back.

A misty ray of sorts came from the object. A thin light-like line appeared, like a flashlight in fog. It didn't touch either the ghoul or me, but connected with the little beast and grew slowly around it like a spreading stain on cloth. Then, as if it couldn't resist, the creature was pulled by the light that surrounded it to the alien's side.

We all stood there for a moment in the quiet of the park just sort of studying each other: me, the ghoul, two alien creatures, and a flying brain. The little monster looked agitated, but could do nothing to free itself from the grip of the light.

The old guy gestured at us. "I'm sorry to have acted the way I did, but we behaved the way we thought you would respond best," he said, placing his hand on the light bubble around the creature. "This little fellow is the last of his kind. They used to flourish on our planet, but as things will happen, they died off one by one. We only recently discovered that they were here on earth also, but again, very few. Their appetite tends to lead them to death."

Mo'Lock straightened up, rigid. "Then he's not one of your people?" he asked.

The alien laughed. "Oh my, no. He's an animal. He will be kept in a zoo, and be seen and enjoyed by millions every year. He's quite an exceptional specimen."

I glanced at the ghoul. He was pissed.

"You mean to tell me you're going to lock this... this baby up in a cage?" Mo'Lock said. I could hear the anger building in him.

I put my hand on the ghoul's arm. "It's not worth it," I said to him, and then to the alien, "I think you should go. We don't want any more trouble. Just leave."

"Let's fuck 'em up, Cal," Mo'Lock said in a low, serious tone.

The alien laughed again, the cocky little fuck. I was almost tempted to do what the ghoul asked. In fact I realized I was still holding my gun and instinctively raised it.

The alien looked at the weapon without emotion. "You act as though your people do not have zoos. They do, don't they?"

I shrugged. "We're not our people. So why don't you fuck off before I shoot your ass."

"That would be most stupid of you," said the alien as he pointed the remote thing up toward the night sky.

There was a click and then a popping noise and above our heads the sky became gray steel. It was the alien's ship and it covered the sky for as far as I could see. Mo'Lock and I stared up at it in awe. I let my hand holding the gun fall to my side.

Then, as if I needed to see more of a show in one night, a beam of light came down and surrounded the alien and the little creature, but not the flying brain.

The alien gestured toward it. "I leave you this as a token of friendship."

"What?!"

"The lobe-tracker. It is a gift from our world to yours."

"I don't want your fuckin' brain."

I was too late. The light was drawing them up and in seconds the alien, the beast, and the ship were gone.

It was just me, the ghoul, and a flying brain.

It hovered over to us and floated in front of my face. I shuddered and backed away, but the stupid thing followed and probed at me with its tentacle eyes. I couldn't get away from it. It was like a giant slimy bee.

Mo'Lock laughed. "I think it likes you, Cal."

I backed away. It glided after me.

"Fucking great," I whined. "What the hell am I going to do with a brain?"

Mo'Lock laughed. "No comment."

No matter where I ran, the brain was right on me, so finally I stopped and sat down on the edge of a fountain. The brain hovered next to my head. I sighed and once he'd collected himself, the ghoul came over and sat next to me.

I looked over at him, exasperated. "I don't suppose you'd mind if I shot it, would you?"

Mo'Lock smiled. "Don't you dare!"

The End

Big Fat
Hairy Deal

# It was June or thereabouts.

I'm never really sure any more. The longer I'm in Los Angeles, the harder it is for me to differentiate between the months. There are no seasons, unless you count rain and fire as seasons. I don't. I'm from back East, where you tell the seasons by the murder rate.

On this particular day, I had been dragged into the woods against my will. I was also showered, clean and sober. I hadn't had a pill, drink, or smoke for almost an entire day. I was completely off my game.

It was Sabrina's idea. She'd finally put the summer issue of the *Speculator* to bed, I'd just come off a series of bizarre cases, Mo'Lock had gone off to Death Valley with some ghoul friends, and overall things were looking pretty quiet for once. Basically I ran out of excuses and Ms. Lynch took the opportunity to rent a cabin in the woods for us.

She didn't tell me about the no-drink-or-drugs catch until we pulled into the park. Believe me, I never would have agreed to such madness had I known.

My name's Cal McDonald. Usually I'm a detective, hunting and killing freaks, and trying to ride a steady, mind-numbing buzz. On this particular stretch of summer I was clean, straight, sober and staring down the barrel of a long, long weekend in a cabin made out of Lincoln Logs. Only two words came to mind: fuck that.

"What you're not understanding is that humankind has spent thousands of years working toward not camping," I said as we walked up a dirt path.

Sabrina glanced over her shoulder, leading the way. "I have never heard a man whine like you, you know that?"

"Wait until we're in bed later."

I was trying to have a good attitude, but my head was throbbing and rattling and my stomach felt like a ball of cement. I know she meant well, but you can't just tear a guy away from everything he knows and loves and not expect some bitching. Shit, this was more than anyone had ever convinced me to do outside of working. I had to give her credit for that. Still, my body had other ideas.

Sabrina walked and I followed until the path all but disappeared. Suddenly I was surrounded by tree branches, pine cones and dirt. Bugs were swarming and for a heavily wooded area, it was fucking bright. All I wanted was a case of beer, something to smoke and my dark house to hide in. This was bullshit.

Sabrina finally came to a stop up ahead of me. I couldn't see a cabin through the foliage, but anything indoors was going to be a welcome change. At the end of the trail Sabrina was standing in a clearing. She was taking off her backpack. I looked around.

"Where's the cabin?"

She looked at me puzzled. "What cabin?"

"You said there was a cabin."

Sabrina shook her head and let her pack fall to the ground.

"You said come to the cabin in the woods with me."

"I said come camping in the woods with me."

I could see she was trying to hide her face from me as she started undoing the button on her pack. She was laughing.

"You lied to me," I smirked. "You unbelievable bitch."

"Consider it payback for bailing you out." She put her hand to her chin. "Gee, I've lost track. How many times?"

She had me. I unfastened the belt to loosen the backpack, but the weight caught me off balance and dragged me backward to the ground. I rolled on the backpack like a tortured turtle. Sabrina started laughing until I bashed my skull on a rock and split my head open. It was totally humiliating. Even Mother Nature wanted to kick my ass.

"Poor baby. Are you okay?"

Sabrina pulled off my pack and started picking through my head like some kind of she-ape. I had a cut from the fall, but there was only a little blood. Once she saw I was okay, she launched back into laughing. I just sat there in the dirt like a discarded puppet and wished like hell I didn't like her so much. If she were anybody else I would have pistol-whipped her by now.

It took a while to get the camp set up; one big tent and a fire pit with folding chairs. By the time we'd finished the sun was already down. And when the sun went down in the woods, it was gone. It was pitch black. And when I say black I mean like no light whatsoever. Damn woods.

We built a little fire and roasted some hotdogs and it was about this time I started getting the shakes. My body was demanding to be fed, but I'd given my word, so I rode out the pain. Unfortunately Sabrina had a different kind of pain up her sleeve.

"Can we talk?"

I felt my heart sink as sweat gathered at my brow. "About what?"

"About us."

Detox and a relationship chat. If there were a cliff around, I would have run and jumped off it.

"Can I have a drink?"

"We didn't bring any."

"Anything to smoke?"

She shook her head.

"How about a pill?"

Sabrina looked me hard in the eyes. "No."

I wiped the beads of sweat from my face and looked at the fire. "You know, I hear there are some plants in the woods with hallucinogenic properties. We could go on a nature walk."

She looked at me, at the sweat on my face and my shaking hands. "Is it that bad?"

"It's been four hours. That's the longest I've ever gone without something since I was sixteen."

She shook her head.

"Don't shake your head at me," I said. "I'm fine."

"Then can we talk?"

I sighed. "Sure."

Sabrina leaned close to me and took my hand. I tried to smile, but I felt my stomach balling up tight.

"There's no simple way to say this," she said. "Cal... honey, you're a mess."

I went from sick to mad in half a second. "What're you talking about?"

"We've been seeing each other for almost six months and I don't think you've been sober once the whole time."

"Define sober."

"Nothing in your system."

She squeezed my hand. "I never said anything before because I didn't think we had anything, but now, I think we do."

"Yeah?" I smiled.

"Yeah," she returned. "But I don't know if I can be with someone who's so self-destructive."

I rolled my tongue inside my cheek. "In case you haven't noticed, more than just my habits are trying to kill me. I have a lot of enemies and they'll be your enemies too if you keep hanging around me."

I got up and walked away. I didn't want to hear another word of her bullshit. I got all of five feet away before I walked out of the firelight's range and smacked into a tree. She didn't laugh, but I could tell she wanted to. That made me really mad. I swung around.

"Look, you knew what I was when you met me!" I said. "Now you decide you like this and don't like that?"

She was shocked and just stared at me like a wounded puppy.

I wasn't done.

"I'm not going to stand here and make excuses. I do what I do because I LIKE IT! Why is that so hard to understand?"

She stared at me. I forced myself to calm down and walked towards her.

"I'm not a fixer-upper, Sabrina," I said. "I come as is."

She just sat at the fire and looked down. I couldn't figure out if she heard me or if she was disappointed. I looked down at the ground and saw something. It looked like a white stick. I leaned down and cursed my luck, my strange, strange luck.

On the ground, undamaged and laying there waiting for me to pick it up, was a perfectly rolled joint.

I leaned over and picked it up. Sabrina was looking at me.

"I swear to you," I said smiling, "I didn't bring it."

Sabrina shook her head and laughed a light breathy laugh. Then she patted the space next to her with her hand. I walked over and sat down.

I held up the joint. "I think it's a sign."

Sabrina laughed. "From who, Cheech and Chong?"

She looked at me until I began to feel nervous and added, "I'm just worried about you."

I stuck the joint between my lips and said. "I appreciate that, but I've been taking care of myself for a long time. I'm fine."

I lit the joint, took a long smooth hit and then offered it to Sabrina. "Come to my side, little girl," I coughed. "Join us!"

She grabbed it and took several short puffs. A second later she hacked and a huge plume of smoke rose from her like exhaust from a locomotive. It was a monster hit.

"Damn," I said and took the smoke for myself while she hacked and coughed.

She had one or two more hits after that, but I smoked most of it and it felt damn good. The shakes calmed and the sweating stopped. Now all I needed was a ride back to civilization and I'd be fine. But that wasn't in the plan. Evidently we were still going to sit around the fire and chat. I did my best to play along, but human relationships are not my strong point.

It didn't help that Sabrina was a casual weed smoker. She acted like a cartoon drunk, wavering from serious to clown-like giddy in the span of two seconds.

Then she had an idea.

"Let's read the bear safety pamphlet they gave us!"

I didn't even get a chance to answer. She was up and rummaging through the tent, giggling like a damn fool. A second later she crawled out of the tent and kept on crawling until she was hanging on my legs. In her hand was the crumpled safety sheet the park ranger gave us earlier. It was a small handout with basic tips on how to avoid bears stealing your food, and what to do if one comes into your camp. Shit like that.

Here's a little tip about bear pamphlets: never read one stoned.

Sabrina thought it would be funny, and some of it was, like the chapter that told you to bang pots together if a bear advances on you. But then she got to the part about bears being meat eaters who like fish and small mammals.

Sabrina looked down at her five foot five inch frame and frowned. "Small mammals? *I'm* a small mammal!"

Suddenly she looked scared. Her eyes went wide, her face pale beneath the flickering firelight.

But it wasn't the pamphlet.

It was the moaning sound coming from the woods.

"What was that?"

I shook my head. "Dunno. It sounded like somebody let the air out of a cow."

"Maybe a wolf?" she said, almost wishful.

"I doubt it," I replied. "Maybe a bear."

Sabrina shot me a look. I had forgotten all about the small mammal thing.

Then there was another sound, almost the same: a long, painful drone of a wail. This time it came from behind us. The first had been from the front.

Sabrina was scared and all I could think was what an asshole I was, thinking I'd get a day's peace. There was something out there in the woods, and I don't know much about the wild, but whatever it was wasn't human.

I pulled my .45 out of my pant leg, and a small .38 custom from the other. I handed the .38 to Sabrina. She took it, bobbled it, then gripped it firmly in her hand and smiled.

"You got me high and holding a gun in no time, didn't you?"

I nodded. "I do my best."

Suddenly the moaning sounds came from all around, and they sounded closer than before. It was dark and we were sitting ducks standing near the fire, so I led Sabrina outside the light and deep into the woods. When I'd put some distance between us and the camp I silently signaled for her to stop.

From this vantage point we could see the camp and the creatures that now stood in the glow of the firelight.

There were three of them. They were humanoid in shape, but completely covered with hair and about seven feet tall.

Beside me, Sabrina whispered, "Ohmygod. Do you know what they are?"

"If they spot us, they're gonna be carpets, that's all I know."

We watched as the hairy creatures tore through our camp. They shredded our bags and clothes and ate all the food. It took them only a couple minutes to destroy and devour everything. It looked like we would be able to wait them out until I watched one of them, the tallest of the three, pick up Sabrina's camera and fiddle with it. Just when the beast had the flash pointed at its face, it went off.

The creatures freaked out.

I burst out laughing.

Bad move.

The two that weren't blinded by the flash spun, spotted us hiding in the woods, and started running towards us. They had faces like gorillas with sharp teeth and flat leathery, black faces. I'd always wondered how these creatures had maintained their legendary status and avoided being photographed or captured. Watching them run at us I began to understand... everybody who ever saw one had died.

I wasn't planning on becoming their next victim and I sure as shit wasn't gonna let them get Sabrina. I stood my ground and aimed at the charging wild men screaming for Sabrina to do the same as I fired.

I hit one in the shoulder and the other in the leg. They both stumbled and slowed, but they didn't stop. Sabrina emptied the .38, but didn't hit a thing. I evaluated our options, then grabbed her and ran like hell into the darkness with those things roaring at our heels.

It was a crapshoot. Either we'd smack into a tree or those things would get us. We needed time to hide. I turned, without giving Sabrina warning, and fired. One of the creature's ears exploded. The other flailed and fell because of the flash. I could have finished them, but I wasn't alone. Time was more valuable than a kill. Lucky for the Bigfeets.

By now, my eyes had adjusted to the dark enough for me to make out where the trees were and where they weren't. I steered us through the forest as fast as we could move, but within seconds we could hear the creatures again. From the sounds of their growling I could tell the third had joined them in the hunt. I could also tell they'd fanned out. Sounds came from behind, right and left. They were going to surround us. They were as smart as they were ugly.

Then up ahead I saw something. It looked like a tower of some sort. I pointed it out to Sabrina, and we ran toward it as fast as we could. As we got closer I could see there was more to the structure, that most of it was obscured by ivy and other overgrown foliage. As we came up on what was a short guard tower, we also saw a long stretch of rotted chain-link fence and beyond that, a bunker-like structure embedded and abandoned in the woods.

"There!" I whispered, and she followed me.

Sabrina paused for a moment as we approached the rusted box of a building almost completely devoured by the woods.

"What is this place?"

I ushered her along. I could hear our wilderness friends crashing through the woods behind us. They were back in the chase. Besides, I didn't have a clue what the place was. Whatever had been in the building had been stripped away. It was hard to tell what it had been but I recall thinking of a classroom or a lab of some sort. It reeked of secrecy and had clearly been unused for a very long time. Not to sound like a ten-year-old, but it felt like a bad place. Some places just have that feeling. It sticks to them like an odor that never fades.

Bad or not, it was shelter from the creatures pursuing us. We ran through a doorway and into a small flat room made of steel that had long ago lost its paint and surrendered to rust and growth. The space inside was wide open. There were no other rooms and no obvious place to hide.

I glanced through one of the windows, the glass crystallized with moisture and mold and age. The three creatures were standing near the tower sniffing at the air, debating, I think, whether or not to go any further. I couldn't see their faces in the darkness, but their body language spelled caution. This was a bad place to them too.

By the time I turned back to Sabrina she had wandered to the very back of the short, flat bunker. The back of the

room had been overrun by a massive tree root and part of the
metal wall was twisted and mangled right into the bark like
the tree was eating the structure and taking its time about it.

Feeling like we might be safe, I edged over to Sabrina
and tapped her shoulder. I pointed to a hole in the wall near
the tree root damage. It would be a tight squeeze, but it
looked like we could fit through and maybe lose the
creatures by disappearing out the other side. She nodded
and glanced over at the creatures.

"They're scared of this place," I whispered.

Sabrina nuzzled against me. "So am I."

I went through the hole first. It was a squeeze, and I
ripped my shirt and pants on the jagged metal edges, but I
got through. I immediately looked back and started helping
Sabrina through, but as I did I saw the creatures at the door
just a few yards behind her. They were coming
in and all three of them had their fierce black eyes fixed
firmly on her.

"Hurry!" I said. "Don't look behind you, just hurry!"

She did good. She listened and came through the hole
without hesitation. She even resisted the urge to look back.
Trust me, I know from experience that those looks back can
be deadly.

I stood and looked around as I helped her to her feet. We
weren't on the other side of the building as I thought. We
were still inside the place, but in a small enclosure. I looked
closer and saw that the hole we'd crawled through had been
some sort of entry. The overgrown tree roots had both sealed
and ripped apart what had once been a door. The
rip was the hole we'd come through. It was the only way in,
or out.

"Oh God," Sabrina whispered, piecing together what I already knew.

We were trapped.

Outside in the main area, we could hear the creatures cautiously moving around, but they were getting braver by the second. I looked at the hole, no bigger than a basketball, but the edges were shredded steel. There was a chance they could reach inside and grab us. There was also a chance, if they were as strong as I feared, they could peel back the tears and come in after us.

I stumbled back away from the hole and my feet kicked a pile of what I wished were sticks and debris, but I knew that hollow sound. Only one thing makes that sound: bones.

I took out my lighter and sparked it for only a second; long enough for Sabrina and I to see the chamber we were in. It was a cell, steel, cold gray with no windows, just the sealed door. There were bones on the floor, whole skeletons. At first glance they appeared human, but the skulls were larger, and the limbs were longer and thicker. It didn't take a genius to see they were the bones of creatures like the ones outside the chamber. But why were they here, and how?

Listening to the nervous snorts and grunts outside the hole gave me some possible insight. If the creatures had put the remains in the hole, I doubted they would be afraid, but if this place had been a laboratory where they were captured, or raised, or grown or whatever the fuck crazy people do with monsters in labs, then that would explain their fear.

I didn't care at that moment, but the idea that these legendary creatures of the woods were created in a lab, or at one time captured for study intrigued me. Sabrina must have been having a stroke. For *Speculator Magazine,* something like this was like finding the Holy fucking Grail.

Sabrina had moved to the corner farthest from the hole, and she was looking at a skull in the pile of bones, a particular skull.

I leaned down to her. "What is it?"

"Look."

I followed her finger to the side of the skull. It was smaller than the rest and right at the temple was a hole. All of the skulls had them. They had all been shot in the head.

"What happened here?" Sabrina asked.

I glanced around the cell. "If I had to guess," I said. "It looks like somebody tried to study these creatures and when the money ran out, they killed them."

"That's a harsh guess."

"Yes it is."

Just when I was thinking warm and fuzzy thoughts about my fellow man, a face appeared in the hole and roared. I jumped and aimed my gun at the face and started to pull back the trigger. At the last second Sabrina slapped my hand. The gun went off. The bang was deafening inside the steel cell. It scared off the creature from the hole, but it also rattled Sabrina and me.

"What the fuck?!" I yelled at her.

She looked more upset than angry. "Don't kill them."

I just sort of convulsed in confusion. "If I don't they're going to kill us, and eat us, I might add."

"I know, but..."

She didn't finish her thought and she didn't have to. I knew.

I touched my hand to her cheek and smiled. I had me an idea.

"I lied to you," I said.

"You lied? About what?"

Outside the creatures grunted and stomped their giant feet.

"When you asked me not to bring any drugs on the trip."

She tilted her head in that "I don't understand what you are saying to me" sort of way that only woman can pull off without looking fake. It worked. I felt like a complete heel.

I tried to look her in the eyes as I pulled the baggie out of my sock. It was full of pills, painkillers mostly. "I'm sorry."

She looked disappointed then confused. "Why are you telling me now?"

The guilt was gone. I wasn't that whipped yet. I smiled and pulled a bag of beef jerky out of my pocket and proceed to empty the meat on the floor, then I did the same with the pills. I placed four or five of the stronger pills onto a slab of the dried meat and then folded and rolled the whole thing into a jerky/painkiller burrito.

By now Sabrina had figured out what I was up to and was busy making the second one.

"Think it'll work?" she asked.

"One of these can knock *me* out."

She just nodded.

When we were done we had three large meat and sedative burritos ready for use. I tossed some of the extra meat out to whet their appetites and they went for it. I saw a huge hand grab the first bit, then heard the sound of chomping and what must have been bigfoot yummy noises.

Then I tossed one of the burritos out. It sat there for a loooong moment then a face came down and gave it a sniff. For a second I thought it was a failure, but then it chomped down on the meat and ran off. I threw the second. This time a hand grabbed it fast.

One to go. I waited, then gently placed it on the edge of the hole in the cell door. A moment passed and two fingers—index and thumb, black and covered with hair—plucked the snack and disappeared.

We sat in the cell waiting and listening. The creatures munched and barked at one another, protecting their food, I assumed, and for a while it looked like the drugs weren't going to work. Then, slowly the sounds faded and turned to grumbling. Finally we heard a gentle thud or two and some heavy breathing.

I looked at Sabrina. "It's now or never, sister."

She nodded as I crawled for the hole, but she didn't follow right away. Instead I watched as she removed her jacket and loaded the bones, skulls and all, onto the spread out clothes. Then she zipped it and tied the sleeves, creating a makeshift bag. I was a bit surprised, but if I published a magazine specializing in UFOs and strange phenomena, I guess I'd do the same.

Still, it didn't seem right.

I didn't say anything. I went out through the hole, easing as quietly as I could. At first I didn't see anything, then as I pulled my legs clear I saw the three creatures sprawled on the floor like a gang of drunks. They were out cold.

Sabrina followed carrying the bag of bones. I pointed to the exit and signaled to be as quiet as possible, then began tip-toeing around the massive creatures snoring on the floor. I cleared one, then the second, and finally the last and was at the doorway when I turned and saw that Sabrina had stopped.

She was placing the bag of bones down next to the creatures. She even placed the make-shift sleeve handle into the palm of one of the sleeping creature's hands.

I just stood there and watched her standing fearlessly over the legendary monster and a rush of emotion came over me. I think I really fell for her then.

It was the scariest thing I'd ever felt.

We made it back to camp with relative ease because the fire was still burning. We packed what hadn't been shredded and headed out fast. On the drive out of the park we gave the ranger back his bear pamphlet and laughed as we drove away.

Later that week, I received a card from Sabrina. Inside was a note saying how much she enjoyed the camping trip, and there was a picture attached.

It was close up of the creature who'd held the camera to its face.

## The End

# A Proper Monster

# Anyone who knows me knows

I shoot first and ask questions at the funeral when it comes to werewolves—or any other monster for that matter.

The first time I met Grimshaw was through a letter I received. It wasn't sent by mail; someone slid it under the door of my Studio City house. The note was handwritten with what looked like an old quill pen. There was no return address and the envelope smelled like lilacs and musk.

The note was short and to the point. Under normal circumstances the content would have meant someone, namely the sender, wanted me to kill them. But this was different.

The note went like this:

*Detective McDonald–*

*My name is Paul Grimshaw. I am a werewolf and it is imperative that we speak about a grave matter that concerns the lives of many thousands.*

*Sincerely,*
*Grimshaw*

The fact that he told me he was a dog-boy before showing up proved he wasn't a complete retard. As a rule werewolves are the least civilized of all monsters, so Grimshaw intrigued me.

I'd let him talk before I smeared him all over the lawn.

It was "winter" in Los Angeles so it rained and there was a little wind. Sometimes it dropped to fifty degrees at night. The way the locals reacted to it you'd think the fucking state was sliding into the ocean, but it wasn't so bad. I liked it. The rain reminded me of back East.

The day after the smelly note slid under my door, a car pulled up in front of my house. This wasn't some Honda Civic, this was one of those block-long vintage Rolls Royce deals with a canopy and a hood ornament the size of a midget.

I opened the front door and stood on the porch while a chauffer, dressed like some sort of gay Nazi, jumped out and ran around to open the door for the passenger.

I knew it was Grimshaw before the door opened. When I saw him I was only a little surprised. I hadn't seen anybody that fancy-pants this side of a classic forties film. He was a tall, husky guy wearing a finely tailored suit, close trimmed hair and—I shit you not—a fucking monocle over his right eye.

I stood on the porch as the regal man approached. He looked completely out of place, out of the past, strolling all elegant and shit down my cracked, white asphalt walkway dividing two plots of grassless yard.

As he reached the foot of the porch, he stopped, clicked his heels and extended his hand. "Cal McDonald. I'm Paul Grimshaw."

"Yeah, I got your note." I gave him the once over, then stepped aside. "Come on in. Sorry about the place. It's the maid's day off."

Grimshaw smiled slightly and stepped across the porch and through the open front door. He was good. He looked a hundred percent human, but he glided like an unnatural. To the normal eye, he seemed to walk like anyone else, but if you looked very close you could see he was hyper-aware of his every movement.

I stepped inside after Grimshaw. He had his back to me and he was scanning the living room. I didn't have to see his face to see he was disgusted. I imagined his office had carpet and red velvet chairs. Fuck that. I like my squalor.

I waited for him to take in the mess and get over it.

"Take a seat anywhere you like," I said, knowing fancy-pants would be appalled at the prospect.

But he surprised me and brushed aside a stack of magazines and sat on the edge of the arm of the couch, his ass covering years of unmentionable stains. I took a seat behind my desk.

"So," I said eager to get things rolling, "what can I do for you?"

Grimshaw adjusted his monocle. "Well, it's not so much what you can do for me, as what you can do for your country, really."

"And I have nothing to fear but fear itself. Your turn."

Grimshaw gave me that one and then got serious. "In 1939 I was sixteen years old. I was born in London, but my father worked as an engineer and we moved around eventually winding up in Germany, where my father worked for the military until he was killed when I was fifteen. A year later my mother passed away as well. I was alone. They were my only family."

"Until the Nazis took you in."

Grimshaw sort of nodded/bowed. "Exactly. Thank you for keeping up with my story."

"I look a lot dumber than I am."

"As you probably know the Ger... the Nazis experimented with the supernatural, the occult as well as unnatural science."

"Unnatural science?"

"The study of the supernatural from a scientific view-point," Grimshaw said. As he spoke he allowed his index nail to extend to a razor point. He scratched carefully under his eye. The monocle was bugging him.

"Yeah, yeah, I'm familiar with the concept... vampires have a virus and werewolves are a mutation of that same virus," I said. "I just never heard it called unnatural science before."

"It was a fairly unpopular term, coined by Dr. Joseph Mengele himself."

"He was really a renaissance man, wasn't he? Just loved to dabble."

I knew all about the Nazis and their brief experiments with the supernatural. I knew they fucked around with a lot of weird shit and I knew they didn't get much in the way of results. I also knew that they did achieve some results, but nothing was ever made public. Well, until Victor Von Fleabag walked in.

Grimshaw went on to tell a pretty tragic story. Evidently the Nazis took him in when he was a teen, but they hardly took care of the boy. They kept him locked up. They beat the shit out of him, and when they weren't kicking his ass, they were making him exercise and build his body up. After a while, when his strength was up and his spirits were as low as they could get, they exposed him to a regimen of strange experiments.

"Most of these experiments were sheer nonsense," he said. "These Nazi doctors tried putting spells on me and had me perform my own ceremonies trying to raise demons and the like."

I lit a smoke. "And nothing worked?"

"Nothing," Grimshaw shook his head, "until they captured an unusual specimen in the forest near Kaiserslautern."

"Bless you."

"What?"

"Nothing. I'm an idiot," I said. "Please go on."

Grimshaw gave me a head tilt of confusion and then went on to tell me that the specimen the Germans captured was a werewolf which had been preying on local farms and villages for years. But the Nazis didn't capture the lycanthrope to help the town, they captured it to use for their own mad purposes.

"You see," Grimshaw commented, "they wanted to see if they could harness the power of the werewolf. They wanted to see if there was a way to transfer what gave the wolf its deadly power into the bodies of Nazi soldiers."

"An army of Nazi werewolves. That is scary."

"Of course the Nazi doctors tried everything to discover what made a werewolf a werewolf, but there was one problem; even though they had successfully captured the creature, there was no taming it and not even the strongest sedatives would put the thing to sleep. At least thirteen doctors were killed trying to run tests on the wolf."

I nodded. "So they'd have to kill it to get inside it and see what made it tick?"

"Basically, but the Nazis weren't about to exterminate such a marvelously rare find without exhausting every possible scenario. They may have been mad, but the Nazis were always thorough."

Grimshaw removed his monocle, breathed on it and wiped it on his jacket lapel. He had a very proper manner about him. He reminded me of the English butler stereotype; very stiff, overly polite and probably the one who committed the murder. I liked him, but I didn't trust him. Not entirely. Not yet.

He went on to tell me what they did to him. In some kind of sound stage or air hangar they created a false wooded environment, a fake forest in a contained area. Both young Grimshaw and the captured werewolf were placed into the environment so an attack would occur as it happened in the villages and farms. The idea was to recreate a werewolf attack in its natural environment and see what the results were.

"You must've been shitting," I said.

"Yes, I was quite afraid. I thought I would die. I had no weapons of any kind, and I was alone against an unnatural predator of extraordinary skill."

"And then what?"

"I was hunted... and attacked by the werewolf."

There was a long silence as Grimshaw remembered what must have been his death. It must have been horrible remembering when and how you died. I know Mo'Lock rarely spoke of his death and when he did, he would usually skip the details.

For the gentleman monster sitting in front of me it must have been painful beyond belief. Werewolves primarily hunt for food, and they like hot. They like the blood flowing and the flesh as warm as possible. To do this they will literally rip a person apart piece by piece, skillfully avoiding major arteries and organs to stave off death as long as possible. People who fall prey to werewolves are usually alive through the worst of it.

"I thought I would die in that awful, fabricated forest, but the doctors had other plans for me," Grimshaw went on. "At the moment I thought I would breathe my last, a Nazi sniper shot the head off the werewolf and freed me from its grasp."

Grimshaw went on to explain that the Nazi doctors rescued him and nursed him back to health. They didn't want a dead man; they wanted a fresh werewolf attack victim to nurture, to bring to full health and then train.

"And you were a werewolf?" I asked.

"Yes."

"How did they control you when you were transformed?"

"Torture," he said. "They tortured me as a man and they tortured me as a wolf with one goal: to join the two, to create a monster with a man's mind, a soldier's mind."

I shook my head. "Christ. Did it work?"

When I looked up, Grimshaw had not only transformed into a werewolf, he had done it without so much as wrinkling his clothes. He removed his monocle and stared at me as he changed his face into a perfect blend of man and monster. He had the eyes and hair of a gray wolf, but not the extended snout. Instead he had a fairly wide but normal nose and mouth. Then he smiled and I saw two rows of the sharpest teeth I'd ever seen.

"What do you think, Mr. McDonald?"

"Looks like it worked."

Suddenly, Grimshaw jerked in his chair. His eye twitched and a sound damn close to a growl rose from his throat. He reversed the transformation quickly and when he was almost all human again he replaced his monocle and looked at me like he was embarrassed.

"I apologize," he said. "That is one of the reasons I contacted you."

I pulled open the desk drawer and looked for something to swallow. I found a couple of painkillers in the pen rack and threw them back. I was feeling twitchy myself.

"After all of these years of controlling my... my state, I have suddenly begun to lose control. I can feel a wildness returning to me. Sometimes I cannot even control when I change"

"That's fucked up," I said. "But what can I do about it? If you go wolfman on me, I'm going to have to kill you."

"Good," Grimshaw nodded. "That is why I came."

"You want me to kill you?" I said, trying to hide how surprised I was.

"That and more."

I nodded and looked right into Grimshaw's eyes. If he was taking me for a ride, it was the best damn job of slapping on the bullshit I'd ever seen. I don't know why, but I trusted him.

He explained to me that if he lost control, he would want me to kill him before he hurt anyone. I didn't say it again, but he didn't have to worry about that.

But then he went on to the next chapter, as if planning his own death was one thing on a macabre checklist he'd completed. He told me how once the Nazi doctors had tortured his wild side into submission, they turned him over to the SS who in turn began exhaustively training Grimshaw for soldiering. They trained him as man and as werewolf, honing skills from stealth kills to all out slaughter, from using weapons and setting bombs to disarming attackers.

It was a long, brutal time period in Grimshaw's life. When it was all over, almost a year had passed, and Grimshaw was a perfect monster. A Nazi killing machine.

"But soon I would discover that I was not the only one of my kind," he said. "The good doctors had created a small army of other soldiers like me. I thought I was the only one because they had killed the werewolf which attacked me, but they had others."

"Werewolves on the battlefield." I shook my head. "That certainly would have changed the war."

"It was not on the battlefield they planned for our use. Our use was for right here, in America."

That got my attention.

"We were trained to do many things. One of them was to hibernate inside specially designed capsules or pods made of the strongest metals available at the time," Grimshaw said and twitched.

"You okay? How about a drink?"

"Do you have a beer? I rather enjoy American beer."

I smirked at him. "Do I have beer? Are bears Catholic?" The joke flopped like a bag of whale blubber. I skulked out of the room and loaded us up with drinks and a bag of tortilla chips. I was kind of starting to enjoy story-time at the McDonald homestead.

As Grimshaw went on the yarn got crazier and closer to home. He saw things in the days before his hibernation that chill him to this day. He saw hundreds of capsules loaded with Nazi werewolves and hundreds more filled with undead SS soldiers called the *scheintod soldat*, which meant something like soldiers who appeared dead or some crap like that.

These capsules were then smuggled into the United States one at a time thanks to the help of some rich and influential Hollywood players, namely an actress named Helga Freed. She played some big roles during the war and evidently used the money to buy "antiques" from all over the world. She would receive all manner of furniture and artifacts, and every single one of them was a Nazi monster capsule in disguise.

"I remember Helga Freed," I said. "She was in that famous picture with what's-iz-face... what a bitch."

"Yes, quite."

I started pacing around the room, alternating gestures between the hand holding the beer and the hand holding the smoke.

"So they smuggle hundreds of these capsules loaded with Nazi monsters into the country, the purpose being to release the creatures all over the states, creating enough murder and mayhem to give the German fucks—no offense—the edge in the war."

Grimshaw nodded. "Very good, Mr. McDonald. I am impressed. That was, more or less, the plan."

"But then what happened? How did you get here? Why didn't they use the capsules?"

Grimshaw smiled. "The war ended and Ms. Freed killed herself, fearing she would be exposed."

"That doesn't explain how you got out of the capsule."

"I was never inside one of them," Grimshaw said watching my reaction carefully. "I escaped from the training facility the night before I was due to be packed away like some sort of fish in a can."

I sat down. I had to think. There were too many factors to shuffle. It didn't help matters that I'd downed the better part of a twelve pack and I was feeling pretty sloshed. Grimshaw was still sipping his first. Some German.

"Okay," I said, holding up my fist and one finger. "We have you losing control of your ability to control being a werewolf, right?"

"Correct."

"And we have a couple hundred capsules filled with similar Nazi aberrations somewhere in Los Angeles."

"Very good."

"So my question to you is... why now, unless this is just about you and the whole control thing?"

With this Grimshaw placed down his beer, adjusted his monocle and stood. "I have something to show you."


We took Paul's car. It was the size of a tugboat and about as fast. Luckily we were only driving from Studio City to the Hollywood Hills so it was a pretty quick trip. In the driver's seat, the chauffer kept glancing at me through the rear view mirror. He had a huge head and sunken, black-circled eyes.

Next to me Grimshaw twitched.

"Where'd you get the wheels?" I asked. It was as much to break the silence as to distract him from his inner struggle. The last thing I needed was him losing control inside the car. Werewolves and closed areas are always a bad mix.

Paul looked at the driver, then me. "It is a rental."

As the tugboat lurched around the winding, narrow roads up into the hills I caught the driver glancing at me more than once. I studied the back of his large head. The palette of his skin was like sick death.

Next time he looked at me I was ready. I caught his eye and leaned forward. "Ghoul?" I asked.

The driver took a wide turn and shook his head. "No sir," the driver said in a deep hollow voice. "I believe the term used is 'fiend.'"

I looked at Grimshaw. "Really?"

Grimshaw shrugged. It was a rental. He didn't care.

I cared. Fiends are the crazy cousin of the ghoul. They do everything ghouls are thought to do: stalk children, eat human flesh, dead bodies. You know the whole Boogeyman thing. They aren't exactly known for being a part of the work force.

Great, I thought. Here I am on a narrow winding road at night, in a car with a twitching werewolf and a driving fiend.

"Kind of unusual for a fiend to be working a job," I said.

The fiend in the front seat nodded. "I am trying to adapt."

"Still eat people?"

"Not for two hundred years."

"No shit." I nodded at Grimshaw.

He nodded back. He was impressed too.

"What's your name?" I asked.

"Lon."

I pulled a card out of my wallet. It wasn't much of a card, just my name, address and phone number with a little graphic of a monster with a target over it. Sabrina made them for me. Because she ran *Speculator Magazine*, she had access to all this kind of shit.

I handed the card over the seat to the fiend. "Give me a call sometime, Lon," I said. "I can hook you up with the local ghoul scene if you like."

The fiend smiled wide as he took my card and slid it into his blazer pocket. "I would like that very much. It would make me very happy. Thank you."

"Well, you keeping your nose clean makes me happy."

When I glanced back at Grimshaw I was feeling pretty damn pleased with myself, but he was not looking good. He was holding his arms against his body, sweating profusely and shaking.

"Grimshaw... you okay?"

"I'll be fine," he stammered. "It will pass. I... it is always hardest during the night."

That was comforting.

Finally we reached the top of the hill. Grimshaw instructed the driver to pull over alongside a tall cement wall that surrounded a gigantic property.  There were hundreds like these all over the Hollywood Hills; huge sprawling mansions owned by actors, directors, producers, and other people with way too much cash.

"Where's the gate?" I asked.

"We will enter over the wall." Grimshaw said, and then turned to Lon standing by the car. "I have no further need of your services. Thank you very much."

Lon clicked his heels and marched back to the driver's side. I watched him as he looked at us one last time, and then drove off, further up the hill. I assumed the road circled the top, then went down the other side. That's the way most of the hills were laid out.

Grimshaw waited for me by the wall.

I surveyed it and knew I wasn't going to be able to climb it, even with a boost. Along the top there were shards of glass embedded in the plaster, so even if I could climb fifteen feet up, I'd get shredded. But Paul already had it figured. He transformed his legs and arms and came at me. I didn't even have a chance to resist. Grimshaw grabbed me, tucked me under his arm and jumped the wall.

We landed hard on the other side. I shoved Grimshaw away. I didn't like the feel of his paws on me. We were in a yard. Ahead was a huge Spanish-style mansion. It was pitch dark.

Grimshaw, now fully transformed back to human, walked towards the house. "Are you armed, Mr. McDonald?"

"Always."

"I wouldn't think there would be reason for any violence, but I want to be sure you come out of this safely."

I didn't respond. What a strange fucking thing to say. I had the feeling he was half talking about outside threats, but mostly he was referring to himself. In an odd way, by asking earlier and now this, Grimshaw had given me permission to kill him.

I didn't give a shit one way or the other. I had entered that "hour since my last drink" stage. The painkillers I took had absolutely failed. I was getting edgy, and I didn't like being led around like some kind of rented mule. Buddy time was over. I wanted some action or I wanted to get back to my place, call Sabrina and get some fucking drugs into my system.

Grimshaw led me up to the back of the house. His manner was pretty casual for breaking and entering. He either knew the place or knew what was inside.

I was sick of being out of the loop. I stopped. "How about you tell me where we are and why we're here."

Grimshaw cocked his head. "The lair of the beast."

"Seriously," I shot back. "Whose house is this?"

"Inside, Mr. McDonald," the werewolf said leading on, "inside you will learn everything!"

I followed Grimshaw begrudgingly up a short flight of dark marble stairs and to a row of patio doors, one of which was open. I took out my gun as I followed the leader inside.

If it was some kind of trap I wanted to at least get off a round before I got mauled.

As I stepped over the threshold of the door and pushed aside a curtain, I saw a gigantic room. It was some sort of library; dark wood shelves lined three of the four walls and went up two stories. At floor level there were statues of demons and devils of all kinds scattered about in between large decorative plants. The focus of the room was split between a grand piano to the right and a huge oak desk to the left.

There was a strange contraption built on top of the oak desk; a shotgun mounted on wood braces with a pulley and wire rigged so that the person sitting in the chair could blow their head off while sitting comfortably.

Above the desk was a large, elaborately framed oil painting.

It was a portrait of Paul Grimshaw.

I turned and lowered my gun on the subject of the portrait and said, "I'm not a big fan of being lied to."

Grimshaw showed me his hands. "I'm sorry, but I had to have you here. I told you everything. I told you the truth."

"Why the break-in routine?" I asked.

"I couldn't risk you running off. I had to get you in here to show you—"

"The Nazi capsules."

Grimshaw nodded slowly.

I gestured toward the shotgun suicide rig on the desk. "Explain that."

Paul twitched and for an instant his eyes flashed wolf. "I was going to end it all, but I cannot do it by my own hand. I cannot die in such disgrace."

I kept my gun on him. "Where are they?"

Keeping his hands in plain sight, Grimshaw began leading me out the room. While we strolled I played with the facts. "So this was Helga Freed's mansion, right?"

"Correct, Mr. McDonald."

"And you were inside one of the canisters after all."

"Correct again."

"But you woke up and broke out and have been occupying the house ever since."

Grimshaw stopped and turned. I took a step back.

"You almost have it right," the werewolf said. "But I woke from the capsule while Ms. Freed was still alive."

"You were lovers?"

Grimshaw laughed, "Dear God, no. She was a hideous woman!" he said. "I removed myself from the capsule—"

"Then you killed the hag, made it look like suicide and took possession of the house, right?"

"Correct yet again."

It made sense, I guess. Despite the fact that Paul Grimshaw was a werewolf, a Nazi, and a murderer, I still trusted him.

Grimshaw continued walking ahead of me until we came to a small bookshelf against a wall in the short hall between the library and the foyer. On either side of the shelf were large black iron candle sconces.

As Grimshaw began to reach for the sconce on the left, I laughed and said, "You gotta be kidding me."

But he wasn't. Grimshaw pulled the sconces and a secret passage was revealed. I was impressed and kind of excited.

I followed Grimshaw down a winding cement stairwell until we hit a really short corridor leading to a large wooden door with a second door made of thick black iron covering the wood. There were three locks: a huge steel padlock and two giant bolts. It was clear that these weren't locks to keep anyone from getting in; any half-assed lock-pick could bust it open in ten seconds. These locks were to keep someone or something from getting out.

As Grimshaw popped the locks, I noticed that his twitching was getting worse by the minute and thick black hairs were sprouting on the nape of his neck. He was trying his damndest to hide it, maybe even fight it, but the lycanthrope virus was strong. From the looks of him, he might fall apart any time.

Great, I thought, I'm heading into a locked dungeon with a werewolf on the verge of a complete breakdown. Good plan.

Grimshaw unlocked the lock and unbolted the bolts and pulled back the iron gate, then used a large skeleton key to unlock the door itself. After a loud click the thick wood door squeaked open and I could see a huge, low-ceilinged room beyond.

Grimshaw stepped inside. I followed. The room was a long cement bunker lined with shelves on either side. On the shelves, stacked five high, were unusually long wooden barrels. They were big enough to hold a man inside them.

Only one barrel, the closest to the door, was open and emptied. This must have been the one Grimshaw emerged from.

"I have been watching over these capsules for many years," Grimshaw said as he twitched. "Now, with me losing control, I want to hand off the duty to someone else."

"What if that someone else doesn't want the job?"

Grimshaw smiled and I could see his teeth were turning to fangs as he spoke. "I had nowhere else to turn."

"They should be destroyed," I said bluntly.

Grimshaw was covered with hair, his hands were clawed. "I realize that now but—"

I shook my head. "You weren't sure it was such a bad idea."

The werewolf looked sheepish for an instant. "They are marvelous creatures... it is hard to destroy such beauty."

By this time, Grimshaw was a full-blown werewolf. So much so that his shirt and jacket had burst open and his eyes had turned wild. His breathing was erratic and drool began gathering at his gum line.

I kept my gun on him. Any trust I had for him was blown to bits.

"I want," Grimshaw growled, "you... to... kill me."

"And then what? Baby-sit two hundred Nazi freak-jobs? No-fucking-thank you. I got enough problems already!"

I could see the dilemma though. The house rested on top of the Hollywood Hills, home of the mudslide and the quickly spreading fire. The place was nothing but soft earth, dried brush and ritzy homes. If we tried to burn or blow up the barrels, the risk of taking down half of Hollywood with them was a distinct possibility.

But it seemed Grimshaw was sticking to his plan: death by detective and let the poor fuck (the poor fuck being me) deal with the mess.

He started coming at me, teeth gnashing, his huge clawed hands poised to gut me. I was ready. He was close. I took careful aim and fired. The bullet ripped the tip of his pointy

left ear and Grimshaw screamed. I removed my blackjack
from my boot and smashed him over the head.

He hit the floor hard, but he was far from down for the
count. I couldn't take the chance he'd get up. I didn't stand
a chance against those claws in a closed space. I hammered
down on him one more time with the blackjack and then
jumped onto his back. He growled and squirmed, but I got
him in a nasty-ass full nelson, and yanked back until his
growls turned to yelps.

The werewolf tried to struggle, but I had him.

"Now listen to me, Grimshaw," I said, "I want you to shift
back to human."

Grimshaw replied with a growl and a lame attempt to
break the pin hold I had on him. I tightened my grip, lifted
his head and smashed him face down into the pavement.
I heard a crack and a single fang slid across the cold floor
followed by a small geyser of blood.

"Shift..." I said, lifting his head, "...back!" I hammered
his snout into the floor.

He tightened up again, but he didn't fight. Instead there
was this feeling in my arms like a balloon deflating.
Grimshaw was letting go. He was shifting back.

I waited until he was all human before I released him
from my grip. I stood. Grimshaw stayed on his knees, holding
his bleeding mouth.

"If you were losing control," I said, "you would've
totally lost it and torn me to shreds."

Grimshaw nodded and stood holding his jaw. He had a
bloody nose and mouth. I looked down and saw his monocle
lying near my feet. I stooped and picked it up. I stayed down
for a second, completely vulnerable, and nothing happened.

When I stood back up I smiled and handed Paul Grimshaw his monocle. "Here. You dropped this."

"Thank you," he said, "but why the smile?"

"You don't want to die. You're just sick of being the caretaker of all this death."

"Perhaps."

"When was the last time you ate a human?"

Grimshaw placed his hand on his chest and opened his mouth. "Human flesh?! Never! I have killed in self-defense, but I have never eaten a person!" He was missing a tooth.

I nodded. "That's what I thought. Otherwise I'd have killed you back at my place."

Grimshaw lowered his head. I was right and it embarrassed him.

"The twitching was a nice touch though. The shotgun rig too," I said. "In fact, the whole thing was a pretty nice production."

Grimshaw shrugged. "Thank you."

I turned away from him and gave my attention the barrels. "Have you ever opened one of these?"

"Good Lord no!"

I approached one of the barrels and surveyed the round cover. There was a latch on four sides. "I think the wood barrel is just a cover," I said, and reached for the first latch.

"I wouldn't do that if—"

I ignored Grimshaw, popped the latches, and removed the wooden cover. Inside there was a steel container with a thickly glassed portal window. Most of the glass was fogged from years of steam and condensation. I couldn't make out what was inside. I used my lighter to shed some light and

what I saw inside was just about the most disgusting thing
I'd ever seen.

But it made me smile.

I turned to Grimshaw. "So, you never looked inside any of
these."

"No... uh... why?"

"Look for yourself."

I held the lighter to the glass so Grimshaw could see the
skeleton inside, virtually covered with fossilized maggots
and mold. Whatever the fuck was in this canister was long
dead. I suspected the same of the others.

I pulled the lighter away just as it started to burn my
hand.

Grimshaw looked like a man who'd just been told he was
going to live, but maintained his very reserved, proper
manner. "Well, this changes everything, does it not?"

"Yes, it does, but I suggest you get rid of these things just
in case."

The werewolf shrugged. "How? Believe me I would have
done so decades ago if I'd had an idea."

I slapped his shoulder. "You're going to feel very stupid
when I tell you my plan."

"Oh dear."


I told Paul Grimshaw my idea and he admitted he felt
pretty stupid considering he'd been living in Los Angeles
since the end of World War Two. But once he'd slapped his
forehead, he moved into action, eager to remove the canisters
from his house for good.

We needed a couple big trucks and some help. I called
Lon, the driving fiend, for the trucks, and a couple ghouls I

knew who lurked in the Hills. We had all of the canisters loaded by three in the morning. By three-thirty we arrived at the La Brea Tar Pits located in the middle of downtown Los Angeles, along Wilshire Boulevard.

The tar pits had devoured countless dinosaurs over the centuries. I figured a few hundred Nazi monster capsules wouldn't hurt.

One by one we unloaded the barrels and threw them into the pits. They'd bobble on top of the steaming, bubbling tar for a second and then slowly sink into oblivion beneath the city.

Grimshaw was officially the sole survivor of this particular Nazi atrocity.

Lon drove Grimshaw home first. We said our good-bye and I told him to stop by whenever he got the chance. A guy like Grimshaw was good to know. He showed me that a man can be a monster but not act like one, and that was a good thing to know.

The End

# the author's bio:

Steve Niles is the current writer
of the comic book *DARK DAYS*, sequel
to his own bestselling miniseries
*30 DAYS OF NIGHT*. *30 DAYS OF NIGHT*,
Steve's first comic for IDW Publishing,
has become one of the hottest titles
in recent memory, and will be made
into a major motion picture. Other
recent comic book work includes
*WAKE THE DEAD* for IDW Publishing,
and *CRIMINAL MACABRE*.

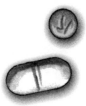

Steve began his career by founding
his own publishing company, Arcane
Comix, where he published, edited
and adapted comics and anthologies
for Eclipse Comics. His adaptations
include works by Clive Barker, Harlan
Ellison, and Richard Matheson.
Steve's adaptation of Matheson's
classic novel *I AM LEGEND* will soon
be reprinted in a deluxe single
volume by IDW Publishing.

Originally from Washington, DC, Steve
now resides in Los Angeles with his
wife Nikki and their three black cats.

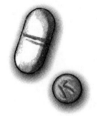

A c k n o w l e d g e m e n t s : special thanks
to the following:

Ted Adams, Ashley Wood,
Brian Holguin, Beau Smith,
Robbie Robbins, Kris Oprisko,
Alex Garner, Jeff Mariotte,
Cindy Chapman, Lorelei Bunjes,
Clive Barker, Korey Doll,
Ben Templesmith, Gretchen
Bruggeman Rush, Jon Levin,
Sam Raimi, Del and Sue at Dark
Delicacies, Mike Mendez,
Mike Richardson, Eric Powell,
Scott Allie, everyone on the
steveniles.com
message board, and my
wife Nikki Niles!

# GUNS, DRUGS, and MONSTERS™

### written by steve NILES
##### illustrated by ashley WOOD

**A CAL McDONALD MYSTERY™**

In the sequel to **Savage Membrane**, Cal McDonald and Mo'Lock are back and this time they're in Los Angeles and up to their nostrils in monsters and trouble.

It will take more than a bottle of hooch and a loaded .45 to get Cal out of this mess.

Written by **STEVE NILES**
Illustrated by **ASHLEY WOOD**

**Available Now**
$15.99
200 pages
Illustrated Novel

ISBN: 0-9719775-2-6

www.**IDW**PUBLISHING.com

Gun, Drugs, and Monsters and Cal McDonald are ™ and © 2002 Steve Niles.
Art © 2002 Ashley Wood. All Rights Reserved.
IDW logo is ™ and © 2002 Idea + Design Works, LLC. All Rights Reserved.